THE CHILD EATER

Brian G. Berry

ISBN-13: 9798596456349
ISBN-10: 1477123456

Cover design by: Brian G. Berry
Library of Congress Control Number: 2018675309
Printed in the United States of America

We shall see that at which dogs howl in the dark, and that at which cats prick up their ears after midnight.

H.P. LOVECRAFT

CONTENTS

ALBERT WALKER

The room was cold, the walls padded and thick. He sat in the corner of his 10x10 chamber, knees sucked to his chest, head buried in between. The jacket secured tightly with fastened buckles, his arms little threat to anybody, but still they approached the man as if he held the strength of a dozen men, able to explode out of the 'safety jacket' they had enclosed over him; which was no easy matter. It took several strong armed assistants and a steady prick of some syringed liquid depressed into his blood stream to calm Walker down. After which, they hauled him into a more secure wing, slamming the door with a solid hydraulic crank of satisfaction.

Albert Walker was something of an anomaly among the residents of Blue Ridge Sanitarium. His history long and shadowed, tucked into the folds of his memory.

A window set into the heavy door no larger than a shoe box gave observers a safer view of the man inside. It contained a solid piece of safety glass and a honeycombed speaker box just below that. A button to the side worked two ways, giving the occupant of that cell the ability to communicate to the observers. But in this case the occupants side had been disconnected. The man inside had an uncanny ability to cripple the minds of his listeners.

There was curious happenings around the night Albert was admitted to the institution.

An after-hours janitor by the name of Carl Cummings was finishing up on his nightly duties, when something stopped him mid-sweep and he stood, almost hypnotized, at Albert's cell on the upper floors, listening to the man speak things, whispering to him. A watchman found him 30 minutes later on one of his patrols. Carl lay spastic on the deck, soapy foam bubbling out of his mouth, his eyes fish-like, as if a great amount of pressure caused his sockets to rupture. It was determined he ingested a large amount of chemical cleaning products that caused a fatal purge of his interiors.

His eyes were another matter.

Another bizarre case that led to the brutal death of Lesley Gwynn, one of the more aspiring doctors on the staff, enabled the final step to require Walker muzzled and to terminate verbal correspondence with faculty and patients. It was told he spoke things during an interview that caused her mind to melt, delirium to control her actions. They found her slumped over her desk, her face smashed into a pile of paperwork, a ball point pen stuck out of her neck; say she jabbed her self numerous times, they counted two dozen holes. When they entered her office a weird piping resonance was heard...she was still breathing, the air working through those jagged rents.

So they made sure to enact certain measures to prevent another of these incidents from ever occuring again.

When being interviewed he would be securely muzzled and could only type out replies textually through a computer—only on rare occasions was he allowed to exercise his mouth in front of others. His food was carefully slid under the door. When allotted time to shower, two shotgun toting uniformed officers kept watch over him, a muzzle, again, fastened over his mouth. To say he was a dangerous man was attributing wings to a devil, they had yet to conjure a term elemental enough to suggest his level of evil. A mind eclipsed in nefarious deeds, a history shrouded in esoteric mysteries.

She took note of his size, he was impressive that was for certain. Even crouched into a ball you could determine the man was a giant. Nearly 7ft, his raven hair dark and hanging in ragged strands, resting over his knees. His shoulders wide, and even with the layer of jacket stretched over his frame you could make out the carved muscles of the man, Albert was chiseled granite.

The female voyeur had a name tag of 'Wilson' pinned to her pristine white blouse, she flipped through a file, clipped to a board, she was going over his activity of the last few days. Leafing through the pages she landed on a 3x6 of Albert's face.

He was a handsome man, so much in fact Wilson grew flustered at the sight every time she laid eyes on him. A hatchet face, the perfect bone structure, a dimpled chin; thick, dark eyebrows. Her rouge colored cheeks warmed over, her pupils dilated.

She blinked her eyes, avoiding his handsome looks and looked at the man more clinical.

But each time she looked into his cold blue eyes, she couldn't help herself. She knew of the mans clouded past, the deeds that were whispered about him. They had yet to dig deep enough to understand how dangerous he was, but it was ascertained through his heinous actions around the sanitarium that he was a force to avoid, especially as the sun bled beyond the hills.

"Seems almost surreal this could be the man who caused all that bloodshed, all that horrible...well, *evil*, wouldn't you say?"

A voice behind her said, startling her.

Wilson turned to face the voice, the clipboard held tight against her chest. A man of medium height, hair the color of dirty snow combed over to hide the receding pate retreating past his ears, thick bushy eyebrows and dark deep-set eyes highlighted by thick spectacles. A sallow face with too many teeth and the complexion of a man who spends too much time under fluorescents. He looked into the portal, observing his patient.

"Oh, Doctor Grant...yes, I agree. He certainly doesn't fit the archetype of the sanitarium, at least the ones above us," she said, alluding to the more incorrigible patients taking residence in their sector.

Grant brushed past her, his face filling the port, his eyes narrowing.

"Has he moved much since you've been...checking on him?"

"An occasional shifting of feet, not much else, doctor."

"I see."

Albert raised his head, looking to the two staring at him through the port.

"Ah, I see my subject is awake after all."

The doctor backed away from the window, leaving an opening to catch a better glimpse of the man. "Tell the orderlies to have him ready by 5pm." Grant said, his shoes and voice echoing along the stretched hall as he excused himself.

"Yes, doctor, I'll make sure they get the message."

Wilson turned her attention back to Walker, who regarded her with vulpine eyes. No longer a crystal blue, but a hard, gunmetal gray. Smoky and feral. Her body shivered, gooseflesh tightening her skin like a drum. Looking into his eyes she felt a mix of emotions from skin crawling terror to outright arousal. It confused her.

What in the hell is wrong with me, she thought to

herself.

Again she blinked away from the man, stepping back from the window.

She believed at times, considering his past, that he must be controlling her, somehow influencing her desires.

It chilled her.

Half the time she couldn't recall how she had come to stand gawking in through the window at him, as if compelled by some hidden agency, controlling her movements. It was an unpleasant feeling, almost sickening.

Composing herself she started to walk away when a loud banging on the other side of the door caused her to drop the clipboard, where it clattered loudly on the linoleum tiling.

Her hand flew to her chest and she crooked her head to the side, her eyes again landing on Walker's. His face was pressed against the glass, watching her, staring into her. Something like a smile revealed a grouping of bunched incisors. She widened her eyes, bent down, scooped up the board and beat a path down the hall, her shoes clacking as she went.

"When is Nathan and Jill showing up?" asked Thomas Combs from the kitchen just around the corner, pouring himself another drink. This was his third for the night. Nothing much, just a pinch of vodka and OJ—a simple screwdriver. But he loved them. So did his wife, Stephanie, herself, feeling warm and alive after two resting in the bottom of her stomach, massaging away her usually strict motherly ways.

"I'm not sure, she told me sometime after seven, closer to eight."

She worried a little with each sip, thinking maybe she should stop her self, but the feeling the drink gave her only encouraged more of the orange liquid to travel along her throat.

Just watch yourself, know how many you've had, and have fun—you deserve it!

She did deserve it, at least she kept telling herself that. It had been a difficult year for her, for *them*.

Another miscarriage threatened to pull them further apart—their most recent one— the second now, was a horrible memory, the effects still burgeoning like an infection that refused to die under the surface. A stillborn that took her hope and dashed it into a pit of ash.

"*Mom!*" The shrill voice caused her to glance up from the sofa to the railing above, the second floor. A head of thick matted brown hair with wide green eyes looked down to her.

"Yes, Michael?"

"Is Robby coming over, too?"

"He is—Jill said he has a new game for you guys to check out."

"Awesome!" Michael turned his head to look behind him, "you hear that Macy, Robby's coming over and has a new game!"

Macy and Michael loved it when Robby came over, he always had something new to bring along with him. Most of the time anyways. Last time he brought over Kerplunk, a game where you had to carefully withdraw thin sticks from a vertical cylinder about a foot tall, staying careful not to disturb the payload of marbles sagging with weight under the nimble straws. Down below were a series of trays arrayed at the bottom. The goal was you had to try your hardest to prevent filling your own tray; the one with the least amount, wins.

"When will he be here?" Michael asked, eagerly.

"Shouldn't be much longer..."

With that, like a blur, Michael ducked away from the railing, disappearing into his room.

Thomas came around the corner, two glasses sloshing around the rim in his hand, the exterior frosted.

"Here you go, babe." He placed one in front of her on the glass coffee table, the other clutched in his hand, sinking back with him in his leather recliner. Stephanie watched as Thomas pulled a generous amount of that drink, his apple bobbing like a piston with each swallow.

"Man, that's good." He wiped his mouth with the back of his hand, setting the glass onto the table. After all these years she still found him attractive. His emerald pearl eyes, his dark chestnut hair, she wasn't much of a fan of his gruff appearance he had taken on as of late, the light bristles of facial hair tickled her flesh with each kiss, and other, more amorous activities.

"Thanks, sweetheart," she tried to sound sincere, tried to push away that gnawing sense of absence in the home, but within she was tormented, defeated.

"Such a beautiful night, maybe instead of cooking in, we fire up the grill, toss those steaks on I been meaning to cook up?" Thomas suggested, reaching forward, grabbing up the drink.

"Oh, that sounds nice. It is warm out there—sounds like fun."

"Great, let me get everything collected, and you just relax and wait for Nate and Jill."

She smiled as he got up, drink in hand, and headed for the kitchen. She appreciated his attempts at showing compassion, he knew what happened to her—to them—tore her up inside, she was stubborn enough to cover it up with a mask of smiles, refusing to speak about it any longer, but maybe she did need to talk about it, to voice herself. *But what good would it do, it happened, move on, get over it! I blamed him and now I'm blaming myself, to myself. He's a good man and he deserves me at my best.*

She raised herself up and headed to the bathroom.

Locking the door behind her, her hands cupped over her belly, a tear rolled along her pale complexion, past her chin and down the length of her long, thin neck. She glanced at herself in the mirror and noticed how much she had aged, even in these past few months. Her normally beautiful copper eyes were dreary, the skin beneath sagged, darkened with lack of rest. Her thick blond hair that rolled past her shoulders looked thin and starved of nutrients, almost in the same condition as her body.

She splashed a handful of water over her face, hoping to cleanse her age away with a more purifying, youthful, countenance. Looking sallow, still, she hopped in the shower, toweling off minutes later and applying make-up to lift her appearance, make her feel normal again. A wide grin pulled her bright red lips apart and flashed a mouth of perfect pearls. She inhaled deeply, exhaling with a low whistle and headed past the living room and into the kitchen.

"Hi *baby*," she said with a sensual grace, brushing a wave of hair behind her ear.

Thomas smiled and moved in close to kiss her.

The lights overhead shadowed his brow with each passing. His eyes forward, focused on the black placard of the name looming closer, Doctor Edward L. Grant, etched into white lettering on the slab. He cursed the name, that man in his experimentations.

His morbid experiments during which Grant would stand back, cloaked in the shadows like some crazed scientist. The blue lighting flickering and striking the walls like lightning from surging volts of electricity streaming along the head and down the body of Walker. The cobbled walls of brick coated in dust, ancient equipment and bottles of unknown fluids and jars stuffed with unknowable things; a piping network of odd tubes and brass machinery gave the room an almost medieval feel. Patients called the room the 'Witch Hole'. Only thing absent in that damnable place were boiling cauldrons, screaming children caged to the ceiling, the sounds of chains reacting to hidden breezes and the hunched forms of cackling fiends.

Some of the guests of the Witch Hole never returned, up and disappearing in the night, their cells sterile, records wiped of existence.

Doctor Grant assured Albert he was only trying to help assist him with the extermination of evil said to inhabit his bones, that plagued his thoughts and actions that drove his salacious lust for blood.

But what Albert felt was anything but a lessening of his instinctual craving for the essence. He desired it more, in copious amounts, to bathe in its intoxicating and fulfilling, richness.

And he wanted nothing more than to tear Grant's skull apart, feeding on the pulpy matter inside with his own two hands, he could nearly taste it.

He was buttressed by two white coat wearing orderlies who wheeled him vertically down the long sterile hall. Both had faces gloomed over with an almost mechanistic demeanor. They hadn't said a word as they strapped him into what was little more than an iron handcart. They both pushed with stiff right hands, the left enclosed around the hardened hilt of the thick security baton. He could remember several occasions when they took the wind from his lungs, shattering his leg bones, even the instance when they nearly deflated his head like a rotten pumpkin with crushing blows as he fed remorselessly on that foul tempered Donaldson in the cafeteria; how sweet was his blood, a young man nary a hair past manhood.

They reached the door, one of the orderlies removed his hand, rapping his knuckles over the smooth red-oak of the door.

"Come," a hollowed voice beckoned.

The door opened with a smooth, noiseless motion, the only sound were of the thick rubber wheels squeaking with each turn.

"Good afternoon, Albert. I suspect you weren't harmed in any form by my loyal companions here, hmmm?" Grant asked, standing at the introduction to his quarters.

Albert looked on the doctor with seething eyes, his words lost in the wide radius of the office. An office littered with reading material, volumes of books crammed tightly within the confines of the towering walnut shelves that covered most of the walls. A large executive desk, neatly composed and cleared of junk and trinkets sat back aways from the door, two area rugs larger than his cell rolled out, centering the room with enough space left to roll out another two equal in width. A globe stood in the corner, canted, a line dividing along the middle, evidence of spirits contained within.

Several sugar cane plants gave a comfortable, peaceful mood to the otherwise grim placement of the office; one residing in the heart of the more uncooperative patients. The ones who would bite into your face, rape you in the cold; the ones who spoke to things in the walls. Most were sequestered to these lower cells for grisly crimes committed during their time with the sanitarium, most restricted from moving about their quarters, lengths of chains tethering from the wall—binding them like exhibits in a zoo. And below it all, notched into cavernous hollows beneath, like a haunted cave sat the Witch Hole.

"Gentlemen, please, unfasten his muzzle, I do believe he will behave, like a good boy, won't you, Albert?"

The orderlies pulled and twisted and manipulated the large buckles that tightened against his face, pushing impressions into his flesh. They removed the device, hooking it over one of the handles of the cart. After which Grant motioned with a tilting of his head for them to give him space.

The two did as directed, each taking a position on each side of the door, their arms folded in front of them, hands clasped together.

"Thanks, doc..." the words dripped like venom from a rabid animal.

"My pleasure, Albert."

The doctor seated himself, using his weight to

shift himself forward, closer to his desk.

"Now, how are you feeling today? You had quite a time last night, do you remember any of it?"

Albert stood there, still strapped tightly to the gurney, his mind reeling back momentarily to his latest encounter with the Witch Hole. He could almost feel the currents racing along his skin, cooking his blood, almost could smell the hairs roasting on his body, and feel his eyes bulging, nearly tumbling out of their sockets.

"Oh, I'm feeling... *peachy*, doc..."

"That's what I like to hear."

Grant gingerly slipped a file onto his desk, leafing through the sheaves of paper heaped within. At the lick of his thumb he removed two sheets hidden under numerous others and said, "I want you to take a look at these, and tell me what you feel now."

The doctor pushed them forward, Walker's eyes fell down, examining the papers below. They were pictures—old prints—not normal photographs mind you, more sketched, penciled-in, the words '**missing** and **last seen in**' in bold print rolled across the top. He remembered them well, his first known victims.

"How do I feel about them?" Albert said, his eyes rolling up into his skull, his tongue slithering over his dry lips, "full."

Grant regarded him with disquisitive eyes, wanting Albert to elaborate.

"I can still taste their innocence, their purity. It nearly gave me the required strength I needed to fulfill my true... *power*," his eyes again rolled upwards into his mind, his thoughts playing out in the grave-yard of his collective tales. His voice was harsh, yet imbibed with an elegance.

"I can still see their surprised faces when I crawled out of those bushes. The slightly elder gal looked upon me with such a sullied face. The smaller one, well she ran up to me, stroking my head, tears welling up her eyes, begging her sister to help me."

The doctor lounged back into his chair, his legs crossed over, his hands steepled under his sagging, pigeon chin, "where were you Albert? Why were you there? How did you get there—so far from here?"

"I was in a great field—a farming community—I was lost, I can't recall after all these years how I came to be in that drab place. What I do recall was that pubescent musk that drifted along the trees around me, traveling up my nostrils into the pit of my stomach. Such a sweet fragrance. From what I recollect it was such a beautiful day. The sun was high, the clouds little more than wisps of cotton, like sheep roaming free in a great pasture. So many leaves, the color of copper, orange and red, crunched under my feet, the feel of it in my hands, its as if it was only moments ago—I can still feel it—taste *them*."

Grant's face was draining a bit of its shade of already a pale, colorless mask. Now he resembled more a ghostly caricature of himself as he listened.

"I wish you were there doc, oh how I wish you could watch as that little girls head tore from her body like, well, it sounds similar to the wet snapping of biting into a celery stick, the way her vertebrae twisted and popped with it, her sweet, warm, nectar splashing across my grin. Her sister screamed something terrible doc, watching me feed on the ripe little girls face, working my tongue up into her mind, holding it over my mouth and letting that sweet warmth lather down my throat. The sister was on her knees by the point, pulling at her long billowing dark hair. Her dress sagged around her like a dying flower pedal. She rocked back and forth, her cries were a sonorous melody to my feeding time. Finished with her sister I tossed the empty skull towards her, it rolled near her, those drained eyes looked up to her, the mouth greeting her with surprise and fear mixed into one. I was always a sucker for art, doc, and it was such a pretty piece. I rose up, feeling the blood inside me, lining my empty arteries and reinforcing me with an energy that I had gone without for so very long. No longer did I feel empty, diluted; no longer a frozen husk waiting for someone to thaw me out, no... I was alive—reinvigorated—with life! And doc, you would hardly believe the length of time I had tasted something so pure; it had been many moons since I felt that way. The older sister, she wouldn't stop bellowing, so I calmed her down."

Doctor Grant sat forward, his arms crossed over the top of his desk, his glasses resting down his long aquiline nose, "and how did you go about calming a girl in such a distressing situation as that?"

"Oh it was quite simple, doc, I merely brushed up against her, swept her off her feet, taking her into my arms and cradling her like a grieving baby. She looked into my eyes with something loathsome, she hated me but something compelled her to remain calm, her eyes drained of knowledge and her face grew tight and pale. She began to suck her thumb. It was incredible! I reduced her to infancy at the site of her sister being sucked clean."

"What happened next, Albert? Did you allow the poor girl to live? Perhaps...shown some heart?"

"Now why would I go to such lengths with that beating, juicy slab of fresh meat in my hands?"

The doctor looked at him, at the soulless monster he believed him to be, that ancient child snatching terror. A creature of some unknown world, the product of demon rites and conjuring pits, wicked, black hooded wilderness cults dancing in firelight, baying to blood-eyed gods and foul, cavernous beasts.

"I merely buried my teeth into her, doc. I bit down something tender. Her skull popped, ventilating the pressure, as my mouth clamped over her. Almost comical the way her eyes drew inward at the gaping crack above her brow. I hoped dearly she could hear the sound of bone crunching and cracking between my teeth. My tongue wrapped around warm, jellied cubes of mind matter, it was delicious. I feasted well. But alas it was not to be, for all the yammering and whining must have carried into the town beyond, someone with better hearing than I must have heard the sirens of terror I caused that little girl, for out of the woodwork a knot of hunters came screaming forward in a wave of rifles and steel to hack me into chunks. Oh I became angry with this, doc, I screamed and howled and demanded they back away or I would return and finish the whole town; threatened to flood their little two-bit hole of a town into an ocean of blood and bodies. They continued forward, probably the site of those little girls on the forest floor drained like they were, causing their collective blood to boil. Clouds of angry led screamed near me, voices of vengeance encouraged their blood lust, it was almost beautiful. But I evaded them, they couldn't keep up, even the dogs they sent against me, tracking my scent wasn't enough. I watched them though, through the trees, authority figures, too, were now out there, torches sweeping the area. No luck, doc. Absolutely no luck. I smiled a big toothy grin as I snickered like a little child playing a game."

Doctor Grant was growing more frustrated as Albert's story continued. Perhaps the image played across his minds eye like an old film reel, the little bodies twisted and used up, discarded like empty sacks.

Or maybe Grant was becoming impatient with it all, wanting to know how the blood seemed to keep him energized for his age. There was no confirmed age of the man, the doctor placed him at or around mid-50's, but at times Albert showed such a remarkable flare and hidden vitality as if he could lower his age at will.

It kept Grant agitated, because deep inside he admired the mans uncanny ability to show such exuberance, as if he held onto a closely guarded secret to immortality.

"What happened next, Albert—to the town, to you?"

"I did as promised. It was a dark night when I moved through the trees, only the moon up above in its silver light was I able to stalk silently around the town. Luckily for me all the little residents were drifting in other worlds, bodies limp with exhaustion, spending so heavy a time in looking for me, waiting for me to strike again. I took my time, with each one of them, doc. I had never been so full in my life. I even took a large amount of them, piece by piece, to my hidden place in the woods. A place they would never find. I gorged for days, weeks, afterward. After what happened to that town, as I'm sure you already know, there was a great hunt established to root me out, by whatever means, mostly tired residents, pissed off towns people, and a group of outsiders, hired and employed by the leadership to find me, hang me, shoot me, stab me, take my head off! Whichever way they could to exact their hatred onto me. They gave chase and I simply disappeared. I could hear them, allot of folk, trampling through the brush, beating around creek beds, shots broke night and day to mark locations where they thought they spotted me, but it was useless, I was always one step ahead. Their feeble equipment and pathetic methods almost caused me to laugh. I even once considered to come out of the trees and help them on their search, that would have a been a riot, they'd probably think I was one of them. Damn fools.

Well, it was some time later when they nearly had me. Chased me deep into a spring, a great vein of mountain water bled near us at the standoff, thick bushes and maples enclosed us; the sun spearing through breaks in the foliage. Now granted they had sent out parties of great caliber and prowess to find and finish me off, though I merely vanished as weapons barked behind me and steel hissed too near through the woods, but this man was different, that man thought he was so much better than I, another foolish mistake. I can still remember that mans name, too. I recall his teammates congratulating him with pats to the back, '*Oh Antoine, you got that pile of merde!*'

Much too early to celebrate. I used another man in my stead, told him I would eat his baby in front of him unless he laid his life down for his family, admit to killing all those children and terrorizing town after town for all those years. I can still make out his face as he confessed to my deeds, those men gunned him down something pitifully. I remember him glancing back and looking to me, at my face. I peered out at him from deep in the bush, before those bullets chewed into his skin, almost made me hungry at the sight. Thinking I had his family, which, unfortunately I did not, I only knew the man had such a family. I remembered his face back in town, how his little girl and boy walked with him and his bride cradled their newborn. Luckily I was blessed with such a sharp mind."

Grant excused himself from his desk, making his away across the office. Reaching the globe, he reached down and with a click the planet halved itself, revealing a bottle of aged scotch and two crystal glasses. "Would you like one, Albert?"

"I'm fine, unless you have a wine cellar buried behind those books of yours."

"I'm sorry, Albert, but I do not possess such luxuries as hidden cloisters of wine gardens."

"A shame."

Closing up the globe, Grant padded back into his chair, leaning back, the glass tipped up, a line of dark amber coursing along his throat. Wiping his mouth with a twitching of thumb and forefinger, he said, "now, where did you go off to after the encounter with those hunters, this Antoine and company?"

"Around. I traveled mostly, in and out of different soils, different climates, up and down winding mountainsides, a customer of various bars, dumps, taverns, hostels and desolate towns, mostly poor, where the authorities wouldn't bat an eye at a missing child. I realized I must keep a cool head and take my pick from, well…the *lesser* of the communities. But one thing I always learned, at the absence of sound-mind at the sight and smell of young blood, was the tempers and ambitions of the destitute, for they took to my trail and drove me out with weapons and steel. I was discovered. Hunted, cornered, so I disappeared."

"But to where? How did you end up out this way, so far from your original home?"

"My home is everywhere, from burning deserts, to misty jungles, to stretching summits, to the wetlands of the moors, holy cities, or boxed in-between padded walls..."

"Answer the question, Albert."

"Now, doc, am I to divulge all my secrets to you?"

"Maybe a trip to...what do they call it...the *Witch Hole*, is in order?"

Albert swallowed, "not necessary."

"Then you will tell me, because, truthfully Albert—Mr. Walker—I would hate to drag you screaming and kicking down there, because I know its not fun. I watch, albeit with a delightful interest, at those who are pulled down there; I see it is hardly a place of fun. So, I plead with you now to let me in, Albert, tell me your secrets, your wisdom—avoid the malice of pain. Because, if you tell me, Albert, I will allow you the simple pleasure of a normal cell, meals outside, books, but I cant offer you the little things unless you tell me—tell me *how*?"

A shrewd smile creased his face, "how what, doc?"

At that, Grant flipped through more of the file, the folder opened down the middle; his fingers running along the print.

"You were found wandering a forest road in the expanse of the Cascades when a single family happened by."

"Yes, I remember quite well—"

"*—a young child, a wife and husband!*"

"They tasted rather tart—too much sugar in their systems for me."

"You were found by a ranger unit passing by, they took you down with several shells of buckshot—pronounced you deceased!"

"Yes..."

The doctor was standing now, growing louder, his voice cracking up with the strain he gave his throat.

"Your body was moved to a morgue where you awakened, killing a pathologist, and assistant! You were then brought down with taser and brought under armed guard out west—to me!"

"Such a good memory, doc..."

"No more games, Albert! No more! It is time you show me, tell me, include me in your world!"

Grant was fuming, each word was punctuated with a pounding of fist over wood, his crystal glass sailed across the room, shattering into fragments and slivers. Spittle bubbled off his lips and dripped down his chin. His face like a furnace.

Albert watched the doctor with delight as he grew red and flustered around like an unruly child, nearly reminding him of little children he peeked and stalked before tearing them into confetti.

"Sure thing, Doctor Grant, if that's what you truly

desire..."

The straps that held tightly to Albert began to bulge, stressing. The leather restraints were heard as jagged fissures appeared down the middle.

Grant watched in wonderment, and terror, as the straps then sprang loose, hanging to the sides like warped streamers. Albert was free, the only thing preventing him from reaching out was the straight-jacket that held tight. That is until he watched closely. Albert's neck broke out in a networking of black veins. His forehead, too, growing tight with pressure. It was at this time when the order-lies already aware something was happening near the doctor came forward, their heavy legs pumping quickly.

Albert closed his eyes, as if he were drawing from some deep mental well, maybe channeling some inner strength, some force. A couple seconds elapsed then the coat exploded in a shower of fab-ric. His face, Grant noticed, was changing, not so much his bone structure, but his eyes, they eclipsed over in a swirling pool of neon red, pulsating like beacons. His mouth it seemed, grew impossibly wide as what Grant thought to be Albert's inci-sors breaking along his gum-line, drew downward like the fangs of some primal animal. The resulting effect caused his mouth to spill over in a fount of blood. It ran down his chin and smeared his cheeks, as if he finished slopping up a bucket of gore.

The two orderlies paused as if struck with a mor-tal terror, but Grant noticed they appeared to be more enraptured, perhaps possessed by some pernicious force, charted through hidden waves. Then what happened next was the last thing he experienced.

They moved towards him, their hulking bodies mechanical in stride, their eyes devoid of compassion. In fact their eyes resembled smoking pits, they were being guided by Albert in some strange hypnosis. They split, each flanking the doctor who was in the throes of retreating, his feet walking backwards, "now, now, Albert, *please*, make them stop."

"But you insisted I show you how I do things, you wanted to be included in my *world*—remember?"

The two looming orderlies came shoulder to shoulder, closing in on Grant who was only a dozen steps from the back wall now.

"*Please! Albert! For God sakes! Make them stop!*"

"There is no God, *here*, doc."

And there wasn't, unless you considered the hideous rites that chanted him into existence countless years before, opening up this world to *him* as being the thing most resembling a god—one of nightmares; of subterranean grottoes full of bloodless bodies and screaming skulls.

His escape cutoff as he thudded into the wall. His hands reaching behind him, his fingers probing and prodding along the surface, hoping for an exit that wasn't there.

Each of the aides grabbed an arm, pulling tight. Grant yelped, his mind screaming in pain that shot around his body.

"Oh, and Grant, before you cross over, your theory was correct—*you were right all along.*"

Grant would have smiled in different circumstances, but he watched with a terrifying reality his conclusion coming alive in front of him. His eyes grew wide with fear and pain, watching as Albert began to fully transform. His bones popping and cracking with the contortions. As if something pounded from within his body to be released, and in hindsight, there indeed was. What he saw as the orderlies tore his arms from his body was the true face of Albert Walker, a moniker he probably acquired from a past meal in some distant state. What stood before him now no longer resembled a man, but a beast. The terror of Europe, the true horror he believed him to be.

The silver balls grouped together in the trench fed into the crimson launcher, spewing across the width of cardboard at intense speeds. Beyond in a further trench, one separate from the other, a grouping of the same balls fed into a similar launcher, it too, fanning out a line of withering firepower in response to the attack. It was an endless battle; balls crashing into one another, the shouts and verbal attacks echoed across the expanse of the battlefield.

"You cheated!" Michael said, raising himself on his knees over his friend.

"No I didn't," said Robby, still squatted below, his hazel eyes moving across the board.

"Yes you did, when I turned to get a drink you took more from my side, I know you did."

"Macy, did I cheat?"

"I wasn't watching. This game is boring. Why couldn't you bring something fun, like last time?"

"This *is* fun. At least me and Mikey think so, right mike?"

Michael was focused. His attention on the cork-screwing star clusters in the middle, trying his damnedest to crash balls into the jagged edges, sending it skittering into Robby's trench line.

"It *was* fun, until you cheated."

"Whatever man—I didn't cheat."

"*Crossfire, the game that pisses you off!*" Michael said, in a mocking, frustrated baritone.

"You liked it when you first saw the box though."

"Yeah, I guess I did; it's a cool box, but I think I'm done playing for now."

Michael, Robby and Macy, had been playing upstairs ever since Robby arrived with his parents a little over an hour ago. Robby, beaming a wide smile on his pudgy face, his dark hair wild like he may have had his head hanging from the car on the ride over, flashed his newest game to his friends. When Michael saw that thick box, with two smiling kids engaging in some sort of combat, the words *Crossfire* spilled across the top, he was ecstatic—couldn't wait to tear it open and start playing. Now he was regretting it. He grew agitated with each game they played—all ending in a loss for him, the obvious factor in his declining enjoyment.

"You're only done because I kicked your ass every game!" Robby said, smiling as he started to collect the pieces and place them into the container.

"I let you win a couple of times, I know—*we* know —how mean you get when *you* lose," Michael said, raising himself up, letting Robby take care of the mess himself.

"Do not!"

"Yes, you do!"

"Nah uh."

"Will you two please *stop*, just shut up already!" Macy yelled, tired of their whiny, small voices, scratching her ears. She watched them argue back and forth for the last half-hour or so and it was getting to her. Sitting there, a mirror image of her mother, growing bored, she finally had it.

"Well, then what do *you* want to do?" Michael asked his sister.

"How about a video game?"

"No, we played them all—beat all of them."

"Well you could still play them even if we beat them," Macy said, rolling her eyes.

"How about we play out back?" Robby suggested.

"As long as we don't get in my dads way we should be fine." Michael said, running to his window, looking down below. "Yeah, he's on the patio, we should be okay."

"Race you to the backyard," Robby said to no one in particular.

They all squeezed through the bedroom door, their feet thudding hard down the staircase; their voices arguing in a mix of slurs and bad jokes.

"*Hey*, you kids be careful running around like that," Stephanie shouted, her face turned towards the tornado of children who blazed through the kitchen in a blur of limbs. The children's voices carried further into the kitchen when they were suddenly cut off and muted by the sliding glass door that led to the backyard.

"Sorry about Robby, Steph," Jill said, her finger swimming around the rim of a half-empty glass. Or half-full, she couldn't remember. She was tossing them back quick. Thomas made great drinks, always had, even something as simple as orange juice and vodka, the man was a natural bar tender, she admired that; among other things, *secret* things she would never let her friend, or her *own* husband, know about.

"That's okay, boys are boys," was Stephanie's tired response.

And boys were boys.

She loved watching the three of them play together, getting along like common siblings, even though Robby was a friend of her children, she felt more like he was her own son each time they had him over. Her best friend Jill, had been bringing him to the house ever since he was a baby—right next to her own—going on twelve years now. They've all been friends since the beginning, since the first streams of life filled their lungs and blood flooded their tiny bodies.

She wished at times that Robby was her son, at least one she gave birth to, it *could* be her son, a second son, like they were supposed to have—twice now.

Three boys and one girl, that would have been something.

"So how are you and Thomas doing, I know things have been a bit *shaky*," Jill asked, taking a small sip of her dwindling drink.

"Oh we're up and down I suppose. Sometimes better than others."

"I understand that."

"Well I don't, I know its my fault, I nag and nag, blaming him for everything. I don't understand why I do it, I just..." Stephanie trailed off, her eyes a screen of water that she was determined to pull back in. "I just...need to stop is what it is. It was none of our faults. Nothing we can *control* that is."

"You are too hard on yourself, sweetie, you need to relax and enjoy what you have," Jill said, pointing to the backyard. "You have two wonderful kids and an *amazing* husband. You'll get through this—together."

"I hope you're right, I do hope so. Because I'm tired of this, tired of being tired."

There was silence between them.

Jill just sat in quiet, her finger still rimming the glass, thinking things. Mostly about Thomas. She didn't want to throw down too much lumber on the bridge that divided Steph and her husband, she enjoyed the chasm that kept them at each others throats, made her time with Thomas much more... *intense.*

Stephanie took the last amount of liquid into her mouth, swallowing it down in a single gulp. She looked onto her best friend, *she is pretty*, she caught herself thinking. It made her self-conscious of her own looks.

Usually down past her shoulders, tonight she had her fire-threaded hair wrapped tightly with a kerchief in a long pony tail, her sparkling almond eyes glittered with energy, probably with a heavy amount of liquor, too. She wore an almost too-low cut blue top, cut into a wide V that exposed a healthy amount of her soft breasts to peek out. She couldn't keep her eyes away and neither could Thomas, she noticed. *She has all the right shapes and particulars that men lust for, and what do I have, some internal curse and bone thin as a rail!*

"Are you okay, Steph?"

Stephanie looked as if she were staring off into some void, some uncharted world that revealed itself ahead of her on the wall. "Huh?...Oh, yes, I'm fine. Just lost in my head."

They both sat in an awkward silence.

"Is there anything you would like to do?" asked Jill, her head craned down, trying to look into Stephanie's eyes.

"Well, I guess we should just wait for Thomas

and Nathan to finish up with those steaks before we plan anything." Stephanie said, rising up, turning towards the kitchen. "I'll go check and see how much longer."

"Okay, sweetie, but don't be too long."

Jill crossed her legs, one hand on her knee, running down her thighs and up past her breast onto the glass in her other hand. Both hands now enclosed around the drink, she smiled a cold grin.

◆ ◆ ◆

Ms. Wilson's low heels clacked along the echoing corridor, passing numbered cells, catching small glimpses of each patient through their port windows, *more like prisoners*, she thought. Each with a history as sordid and grim as the last.

She had been dispatched on a small errand at the orders of Grant, checking on the status of each patient, making sure all were accounted for and not currently in the throes of self-harm—or worse —which was common in the '*catacombs*' as her colleagues referred to the lower echelon of the sanitarium.

She wondered why the orderlies couldn't do it, but then quickly dismissed the notion, knowing they would be keeping an eye on that beastly man, Albert. Doctor Grant kept his wing isolated, away from the curious eyes of meddling staff on the upper floors. Entrusting his protege, Ms. Wilson and the two hulking strong arms, Earl and Harold, to keep an eye on things; keep things running.

They never left his side, even down in that room below, where she shuddered to think of; such a ghastly place. It reminded her of haunted basements and diseased pits. She had imaginings of what happened down there, the cruel treatments, mad experiments; at times she could hear those blood curdling screams in response to some unknown torture being meted out in the darkness of that charnel house.

Grant grew angered at her attempts of probing his research. He wouldn't divulge much of his methodology to her, oftentimes reacting like a rotten child who refused to share. He insisted that it was beneficial to his studies and well intentioned to the betterment of the patient.

But she gathered enough of her own evidence to suggest horrible things took place in the confines of that place; whispers of dreadful deeds leaked from victims of the Witch Hole, scratching up her spine as she walked along those lonely passages. Faces tight, anticipating a portent to an unspeakable terror, painted the faces of men and women, dragged in chains along the corridors, forced into the hole.

She could remember an instance where a man was being led away—dragged—down the hall outside her small office, she listened as his nails screamed like knives over chalkboards and his screams were nearly enough to cause her hair to gray over.

There were many times she would remain up at night in bed, rethinking her position with Blue Ridge, and tonight was the night she bee-lined over to Grant during the closing of his appointment with Albert, informing the doctor of her decision. She was uncertain how he would react to the news, she felt an unease speaking to him anymore, something behind his eyes akin to madness boiled and stewed awfully—it terrified her.

She was full of hope the first day she entered the facility, welcomed warmly by the faculty. But as time moved on she saw the sanitarium for what it was, and she could no longer walk the dismal halls without trembling down the steps to her new assignment. Like descending down an ancient passage into some blighted cavern, choked with cobwebs and child eating ghouls.

Driving along the winding and climbing route of evergreens to reach Blue Ridge in itself was a chore, especially during the winter months, where a lick of snow could cause you to slide over the road and tumble down the mountainside, possibly to never be discovered in the thick ocean of spruce below. Swallowed by nature.

The building inspired images of condemned mad houses, haunted by specters of malevolence and chaos. The kind of abandoned hospitals you read about in thrillers or learned about in documentaries.

Her final decision came to her as she took notice of Grant and his strange behavior of the past months. Something took residence in him, something alien and confounding. She couldn't quite piece it together, but his mannerisms, his behavior, had become shocking.

At first he was a welcoming gentleman, a nice teacher and educator, one of the more senior fellows with precedence and authority. But something took hold of him, some unseen intrusion.

It happened around the time Albert was admitted to the grounds.

He became foul and explosive with emotions. His complexion withered and dehydrated. His eyes bloodshot and glassy.

He became obsessed with old texts that he refused to share with her—with anyone. There were times she would near his office and hear strange things being muttered, almost as if he begged, pleaded, for something; a whimpering conversation of hushed, illusory syllables. Albert made frequent appearances in his office, too. At odd hours, especially on nights with silver moons and ebon skies.

She became terrified most times, but tried her best to keep her demeanor from compromising and revealing her disgust and fear of the sanitarium and the doctor.

But it became too much, eating away in her mind. Now would be the time to take her leave, establish herself in a more reputable practice, away from the howling woods and screaming patients, crazed doctors and cavernous hollows into unknowable places.

As she continued forward something up ahead gave her pause. The clipboard held tightly across her chest, she brushed a strand of hair that fell across her cheek. "Hello?"

Her voice carried down the corridor, "*hello*?" Her timber grew anxious—a hint of annoyed fear. A figure quickly ducked around the corner up ahead. She caught only a fleeting glimpse of a long coat. *Probably Grant*, she thought.

She hurried her steps, the smacking of her heels pounding madly down the hall.

Can anyone around here have the simple courtesy of a response.

As she neared Grant's office, she noticed the door slightly ajar. A wedge that gave a small glimpse into the room. "Doctor Grant," she said hesitantly, as she gently eased the door inward.

The sight spilled out in a gruesome gasp. The clipboard clattered to the ground, papers fanned out beneath her. Her hand flew over her mouth in revulsion.

"Oh my God!... *Help!*"

She forced herself into the office, not getting more than a few feet when she took a step back, unable to move further into that massacre. Her throat began screeching for help, she reached for her phone when she remembered that Grant confiscated all forms of communication before anyone took a step into his wing.

Her eyes darted back and forth over the scene,

the two orderlies seemed to be a mixture of broken body parts, a jumble of discordant pieces of biology, something you would see in the aftermath of a bombing. Splashes of blood covered the walls and furniture as if painted by a macabre, abstract artist. The face of the doctor looked upon Ms. Wilson with a shocked scream, his jaw locked open, one eye sunk deeper in the skull than the other. She shrieked at the site, his arms and legs had been torn off. Only something capable of producing incredible force would be able to pull the arms and legs from a man as freely as a little child tearing the limbs from insects.

Albert...

Albert was gone! At least he didn't appear to be slopped among the remains.

A sudden scream clawed into her soul, causing her blood to go to ice.

It came from down the hall. A mans scream, one full of horrible agony, a death cry.

She backed away from the room, hugging the frame of the door. She made to peak around the corner, ensuring it was safe to step out.

She stood alone, frozen, her heart hammering against her chest bone.

She took a step and the sound hit her ears like a gunshot.

Her *shoes*, they would give her away.

She kicked them free and padded softly down the corridor. Coming to the corner, she dropped to a knee and peaked around the bend.

A body.

It was the security officer who stood watch and escorted staffers.

Even from the the distance that separated her from the body, she could clearly see a widening pool of blood pouring out of the man.

She ducked back away from the corner, tears spilled down her face, her hand muting the scream that wanted to come, that wanted to release and shatter windows.

I need to get out of here, she thought. She couldn't sit around and wait for whatever caused this to happen to her. She had to get to that office, maybe grab something she could use as a weapon—and grab her phone.

She forced herself to stand and rounded the corner, keeping close to the wall she slid quietly along. The body fully visible, the damage was gruesome. His arms, like Grant's, were cut clear through, his head looked detached but in place, hovering slightly past his bloody neck. One leg remained on the man, the other tossed against the wall. Whatever was used on the man was sharp, enough to cut steel with a single swipe.

Marion, he was such a sweetheart.

She did her best to avoid laying eyes on the man, fighting the bile that ran up her throat. Images of screaming death faces and mangled limbs, twisted skin, and steaming puddles of anatomy, nearly caused her to buckle over and release the horror that knotted her stomach.

She noticed the security door had been left open. Probably Marion coming to investigate the lone figure—Albert—walking down the hall on the security monitor. He kept a close eye on things in the catacombs, personally selected by Grant to prevent unwanted intruders from roaming freely and gaining access in his sector.

She eased up to the door and moved inside. Reaching the desk, she glanced over the monitors. All the patients seemed to be asleep, she noticed the time, *6:11pm*. Odd, but not unusual from all the drugs administered to them running through their blood stream.

She followed the monitor that looked onto the main door leading to the upper levels, it had been forced open, a series of what appeared to be tears the shape of thunderbolts scraped down the middle. The sight again caused her to shiver.

She noticed the red phone that communicated to the security office on the lobby floor. She hastily scooped it up, "hello! Anybody? Please, help!" She was greeted with dead air. No response. She slammed the phone down in protest.

She began to pilfer through drawers, looking for keys, some way to open the security cabinet that housed her phone and purse. She realized in her haste that the keys would undoubtedly be with Marion. She coughed up a wad of something spongy at the thought.

Moving back out into the corridor she approached the remains, squinting her eyes to shut out most of the details, she looked to his belt, noticing the metallic sheen of the key-ring. With a quick motion she snagged them from the clip, jumping back in reaction as she felt his warm blood on her fingers.

Quickly she fumbled around with the keys, fitting each one into the lock until the right one popped with a click. With the heavy steel door opened she reached inside and retrieved her phone and purse. No weapons were stashed within. Only a taser shaped like a pistol, coated in yellow paint with black stripes. She grabbed it, unsure of how to even use it, but figured it was better than nothing.

She checked over the monitors to confirm she was the only one left on the ground, that no wandering phantoms would snatch her from the shadows as she stepped outside of the security office. She tried the phone, but it was useless this far down.

She side-stepped around the pile of gore, making her way up the steps. She reached the door, moving inside the hall that connected to the elevator that sat a ways back. Seeing it was clear she ran down the short corridor until she reached the elevator, punching the key with nervous fingers. The other hand wrapped bone white around the taser gun. It was trembling in her hands from the adrenaline that pumped along her body.

The door pinged open, she moved inside, smashing the key pad for the lobby level. *Almost out of here...*

It was a tense 30 seconds of machinery churning gears along that shaft, her thoughts racing and reflecting on all that blood and body parts. She couldn't imagine a person strong enough to rend limbs from bodies and rip gashes in doors.

He must have gotten hold of some implement, probably stalking the halls of Blue Ridge now, cutting into the flesh of others. Maybe waiting for you up top, waiting for the door to open up. He'll grab you, pull you into him, his body pressed against yours, the blade spilling a hot sensation up your spine—stop it!

She braced herself as the door whooshed open...

A sound bounced around his ears. Something up ahead beyond the clearing drew his attention.

The woods behind him were a knotted mass of spruce and assorted firs. The moon glimpsed through breaks in the boughs above resembled a giant silver eye, casting a ghostly pallor to the pine needle ground under his feet. The stars tore across the sky in fleeting shows in between thinning clouds. Shadows deep in the thickets obscured his progress. A breeze winded by, rustling the branches around him.

That sound again, it was a hollowing sound, a faint echo. Repeated with a drumming regularity.

As the columns of pine separated, becoming less congested, a fluttering of movement caught his attention. His eyes narrowed, becoming focused. His nostrils flared in and out.

There was a shining radiance above them, two forms running in circles, close together as if after something. The hollowing sound became flat, now a heavier thudding, slapping noise, as he moved closer.

Voices, two distinct in tone, berated one another, mocking, insulting and encouraging. Several stretched poles topped with light wrapped around the perimeter of a small arena of cement and dividing lines. On each side stood a curving pole with a basket of silk threaded, hanging limply. As Albert slid to the edge of woodland between the court and him, the lights gave description to the forms.

Two men, chasing around a ball, orange, and leather, crisscrossed in black seams, tossing it into a netted basket above, followed by shouting and laughter.

Albert, crouched low against a thick stalk of pine, his stomach spoke and twisted with a pervading hunger, his eyes staring ahead menacingly.

His nostrils pumping in and out, drool bubbling out of his mouth, driving streams down his pale chin. His skin tightened, threatening to burst apart in bloody, fleshy fragments, shredding that human sleeve, that costume he wore to conceal, and ingratiate himself around the peopled pastures; walking amongst fields of laughing meat, meat that screamed and laughed, and bled—lots of blood.

His predatory instincts grew impatient, his lips

reeled back between grinding teeth, desperately wanting to reach out and pull the two young men into the woods and tear holes into them, listen to them scream and holler as he fed. It was much more fulfilling—and appetizing—while they were alive; still kicking and fighting. An all but useless gesture, a flight mechanism lacking the will to stave off the fury of what hides in the bowels of which calls itself Albert.

Walker topped the chain of nature, scurried up and conquered the beasts that stalked the wilderness, darkened jungles, desert wastelands and cityscapes.

Once upon a time, had reduced distant hamlets and villages to ossuary pits and gore saturated crypts. Raiding communities of their futures, snatching away into dark recesses to the tortured cries of shattered parents.

Though he was closely related to nature, in some obscene manifestation of mimicry, what rooted around inside was an aberration, something corrupted, tainted; conjured from old rites and casted to life by elementals and burning pyres—a scourge to plague lands with misery and terror. And here he was in the shadows of a quaint suburban municipality with manicured lawns and two story homes, enclosed in rolling hills of green timber.

"*Hey!*"

Albert winced, his thoughts derailed as he thought he had been discovered.

"You ready to finish this shit up?" the voice said,

belonging to the taller of the two. He wore matte blue shorts with white stripes on the outer leg area, a white sleeveless top pasted to his skin with sweat, his hair short and even from Albert's distance he could make out a coating of perspiration reflecting off the man.

"Yeah, only if you think you can handle it," came the reply of the other man. In a near matching set of sports wear, his shorts dark, grayish. His hair a bit thicker, plastered to his head.

The ball bounced and bounced, crashing to the pavement with more speed as the two chased one another round the court. Albert watched, scheming, formulating his own game, he could nearly taste the victory.

"Hey dude, stop crowding me," gray shorts said, hunched and keeping the ball close.

"I'm not, man, just throw the damn ball already."

"Get off my nuts, asshole."

Gray shorts ducked out of the defense of his taller rival, leaping and reaching up, letting the ball roll from his fingers. It sailed up then smacked the backboard, followed by a roaring laughter from Blue shorts.

"It was your fault, you had me all choked up."

"Whatever, stop making excuses."

"*Hello?*" a voice said, putting an early stop to their bantering.

Albert came down a small field of grass that lined the gap between the woods and park.

"Hello?" Gray shorts said, a confused look on his

face. The ball resting tightly under his arm on his side.

"Hi, sorry to bother you two, but I was curious if you saw a small little pup wandering freely through the park, perhaps he came by and paid you a visit?"

The two youthful men gave the man who emerged from the trees a bewildering, puzzled, glance. Wondering what to make of him, something seemed off. He was in tattered garments, almost like scrubs or patient garbs. His sleeves looked torn as if he reached into a jagged hole, shredding the cloth. But he was a big man, thick and hulking, a crazed look to his eyes, glassy and wet. His hair ruffled and stringy as if it hadn't been washed, or was sticky with something.

"Nah, man, haven't seen no dog around here," Blue shorts said, taking a step back, like the odd man gave off a rank odor.

"Ah, a shame. He is an impertinent mutt. I'd hate to lose that one, been with me since he was but a small lad, a tiny pup, like you," Albert pointed to Gray shorts, which caused the ball to slip from his grip.

"What's that supposed to mean, old man?" his fists balling up at the insult.

"I mean nothing of it, but that you appear to be quite stringy, not allot of meat on those bones, but what meat I require, your friend here will undoubtedly offer," Albert briefly turned his attention to Blue shorts, before centering his eyes on Gray shorts again. "Besides, you have plenty of marrow in those tight, tiny bones..."

The two took several steps backwards before turning fully around and breaking out in a quick run to the small parking lot. A single car sat bathed in the night alone.

His jaw tightened, his muscles corded, Walker loped after them, enjoying the hunt.

"*What the fuck man, he's right behind us!*" Shouted Gray shorts.

Both were aligned in flight and panic. Their hearts screamed against their chest, the smaller one was in tears. Blue shorts panting, his own eyes flooding over at the thought of some strange man who came from the woods now chasing them, speaking of meat and bones.

That funny feeling he had earlier was something primal, he felt it instantly, radiating out in unseen waves. He knew that man was trouble, and now they were beating through the grass, hoping to avoid falling into the grip of that man.

"What do we do?" Gray shorts shouted out, his voice chalky and terrified.

Before he could get a say into a possible course of action, something happened. His friend was no longer at his side. A second ago he was screaming, then silence. Blue shorts slowed his pace when he noticed it. Looking behind him, around him, to the side, "*Mason!*"

But Mason didn't reply. Again Tyler shouted, "*Mason!*"

There was a small grunt, enough for Tyler to

glance to his side. Out near the restrooms, he heard a struggle. Like someone being smothered, dragged away with a meaty hand clamped over their mouth.

"Mason?" It was a spooked cry, like he wasn't sure what to think. He couldn't abandon his brother like this. He had to do something, but was nearly immobilized with fear. He threw his hands up to his head, fingers interlocked, pulling his hair.

"Mason!"

Nothing.

He thought maybe he should go for help, but dismissed it, he needed to help Mason himself—right now.

"Help! Somebody!"

Greeted with a deathly silence. Not even the crickets chirped no longer. It was an eerie vacancy, permeating with dread, his mind flickering through scenarios of cannibalistic mountain clans shucking meat from young bones, sharpened teeth tearing viscera in dripping flaps.

He nearly broke down as his legs gave way to jelly and he fumbled with shaky hands with the keys in his pocket, unsure of what to do. A blood choked shriek nearly caused Tyler to drop in a palsied heap of quivering limbs. *Mason...*

"I'm...I'm coming..." Tyler stuttered.

Something inside of him told him to help. Whatever courage he held on to worked its way into his thinking; his arms and legs. He made for the restroom.

It was an expanse of red brick, two openings gave

way to a man and womens side, a drinking faucet in the middle. Across from each other, the entry's were hooked in L shapes so you had to walk up and down then round into the facility.

Two large trees gave shade to the building in the daylight, but tonight was dark, even with the shimmering of the silver moon above, the night grew sinister.

Tyler thought the trees he was well familiar with, accustomed to from numerous visits to the park, now resembled shadowy things with leafy fingers, waiting to grab him, take him up into the branches.

His heart wound to the point of rupture, his vision blackened, fluttering with patches of blur and spots. His legs wobbled and felt heavy with each step.

He left the grass and now stood on the pavement; the bathroom looming before him.

"M-Mason?"

A slight breeze was the only response, the boughs above trembled with a rustling.

He nearly gave up and went to turn when a low bubbling, wet noise, made him shudder. The sounds were sloppy, like a dog lapping up leftovers off a plate.

There was a thin trickle of blood that wound in a slithering pattern into the mens side.

Everything inside him now screamed for him to run, to turn now and get help. He didn't want to go in there, not really. He knew what he would see, what was in there, and it would haunt his days. But he had to, almost a morbid sense of confirmation, an inquisitive afterthought. He followed the bloody trail as it snaked into the darkened bathroom.

He stopped just as he came to the rectangular entrance. It was black.

A portal; something that planted ideas of yellow smiles and red eyes reaching out to you with hooked claws and pulling you into murky places.

He stood frozen, unable to move any longer. Something caught his attention, some faint movement. He reached inside to flip the light switch.

The snapping sound was almost too much for his already fragile state.

No light came forth.

He clicked it down, then back up; several more times in frustration.

That's when he saw it.

There was light, but this light was unnatural. Glowing, blood-red nodules close together—eyes. They narrowed and boiled as whatever those eyes belonged to snarled in the dark.

Instinctively, Tyler went for the light switch again, his fingers flipping maniacally over the toggle.

There was a flickering, the light above popped and sizzled, illuminating the horror show beneath.

It was the old man, or what had become of him, because now he no longer resembled anything remotely close to the evolutionary tree. This thing, though possessing human qualities, had a terrible grin with dripping fangs, fangs that busied with his brother.

Mason lay in a pool of himself, shredded into a pile of discarded meat and bone, no longer recognizable as the thing fed.

The thing had an almost bestial snout that tore the visage of the old mans face in a useless mask that hung in flaps at the sides of its—his—new face.

The light popped again, flickering off the scene in a macabre show of strobing that ran up his spine, then above a fountain of sparks closed the room in a gloomy shade, this time drowning the scene in a haunting blackness.

Tyler seized up and screamed something akin to a wailing baby watching its mother be tortured.

He turned to run when he was caught on something, something with hooked fingers and black nails that cut steel and rend flesh. A guttural, throaty, beastly cry erupted within the small confines of the restroom as it took Tyler into the darkness.

"I was not."

"Don't deny it; I saw you, and it wasn't by accident, *Thomas.*"

"Babe I think you had a little too much tonight, maybe you were seeing things that weren't there."

"Don't begin to put blame on my little...*problem*...up there," she said, pointing to her head, an acidic edge to her voice.

She had been dealing with a series of panic attacks and crippling anxiety ever since her last loss. It stewed and brewed something bad in her mind since the first one, the second dropped the gates, let go the flood of pent up emotional tolls, and went to war with her mind. Laying her up in bed for days at a time, shivering, alone, hoping to clear her thoughts. Other times an overwhelming sense of suffocation, of fragile senses, the slightest touch causing her to jump and seize up. It was debilitating to say the least.

"I'm not honey; honest. Look, I'm sorry. I really am, I will admit I did catch a glimpse—"

"—or two..."

"Or *two*, yes. I *am* sorry. You forgive me?"

He reached a hand over to her, rubbing her leg, his fingers moving along her inner thigh, it felt good. Spread a warmth down there, a tingling sensation that caused her to blush slightly.

She was trying, but knowing he was staring at her chest, *more* than a couple of times, was a bit too much for her. She already felt impotent in comparison to her friend. And those weird looks Jill gave her husband only accentuated an unease in her bones over the two of them.

"I'm sorry, I'm just... not feeling *right* tonight. My stomach hurts."

He pulled his hand back, placing it on the steering wheel. His face showed disappointment, maybe frustration at his attempts to touch her being rejected.

He stole a glance over to her, noticed her holding her stomach again, lost in her mind probably, staring out the window into the black night.

They were just passing Sherman Park, only a couple more blocks to go and they would pull into the drive of their home.

He noticed a single car out in the lot, nobody around. Then drew his eyes to the digital clock on the dashboard, 7:45. *Probably a couple of teens fooling around in there*, he thought. He could remember the many nights he shared with Jill, alone in *his* car, parked in dark spaces of the city. Besides the car, the park looked dead...

After Jill and Nathan left, Robby stayed behind after pleading with his parents to allow him to spend the night. The Combs already agreed he was more than welcomed to stay over, Michael and Macy had a helping hand in that one. They decided to head out to Sunset, a local market, the only one that allowed movie and video-game rentals off their shelves. They told the children they could each pick out one movie or game for the night, something to keep them entertained and out of their hair.

It was a small market, been there before they started their lives in Court Springs, a small suburb, isolated in a wash of evergreens. It was a great place to start a family, so they put their finances together, signed a sheaf of papers and settled down.

"I can't wait to get home and check out these movies," said Michael, going over the back of the DVD. The title read: *The Basement, a tale of mutated horror*. The cover grabbed his attention. A darkened cellar with glowing green eyes and a giant, clawed hand coming out of the inky blackness. The font a dripping blood. It was great.

The other title: *Ghost Shark*, one of those horribly executed shark flicks that you just had to love. Supposedly has a scene where a guy is sitting on the toilet and, according to the quote, *"there are worse things out there to help you wipe."* It had more cheese than a cheddar factory, but that's what they enjoyed. Their parents thought it ridiculous, but, they agreed to it.

The last movie they picked out was a title about a group of blood sucking vampires living out of a cave in some sea side town of Santa Carla, looked promising.

"Which one do you want to watch first?" asked Robby, checking out the cover to *Ghost Shark*.

"I'm thinking *Ghost Shark*," said Macy.

"Yeah, definitely *Ghost Shark*," agreed Michael. "I'm wondering about the toilet scene," he laughed.

"Looks pretty funny, really," Robby said, flipping over the case. On the cover was a translucent great white, wide open jawline, in the middle were the faces of screaming children.

"I don't know how you kids watch such garbage," said Thomas up front, his eyes on the road ahead.

"We just do dad, its good stuff, maybe you and mom should watch some of these some time. You might really enjoy it."

"I think not, Mikey, maybe if there was absolutely *nothing* to watch and I was *beyond* bored, then yeah, I might give it a go."

Thomas eased the car over the curb of his driveway, pulling to a stop. Four doors opened simultaneously, closing around the same time. Footsteps hurried to the front door as the three children, high on sugar and excitement, clutching the rentals waited eagerly for the front door to open.

Thomas attempted to wrap his arm around Stephanie, who brushed his arm away with a cold hand.

Albert looked up from his meal as in reaction to an invader in his lair. The sound of a motor, and tires crunching pavement, caught his attention. His teeth and snout covered in shredded flesh and bloody meat. His nostrils went hyper, something caught his scent. Some effulgent redolence. It was sweet and ripe, harnessing the life essence that would bear the harbinger of his long dormant wrath to uncoil out from its slumber. It's been so long...

◆ ◆ ◆

"How many did you count?"

"I've counted 3, from what I can ascertain, that is. Harper scratched off 5 more, that he's sure of that is."

"Jesus Christ, a goddamn bloodbath. What's with the woman?" the newly arrive detective wanted to know. She was sitting on the last step of the stairs that led into the building.

"Oh, she was the one who rang for help, says her name is," the detective went for his notepad, "Irene Wilson."

"What's her position here?"

"An assistant, she told me, not much else."

"Thanks, Simms."

Detective John Miller was called up just as he was about to head out of the office for the night. A Friday of all nights. Some horrible occurrence out at the aging madhouse up on the hill needed his attention. Reluctantly he made his way out to the old sanitarium, curses leaving his mouth most of the way up the winding road. He had plans, he didn't need this shit tonight, and he most assuredly would close this situation up fast so he could get to the comforts of home, away from the usual bullshit of dead bodies and blood spattered walls.

"Mrs. Wilson?"

"Ms...Ms...Irene, Irene Wilson," she said, her eyes distant, lost in some other world.

"Ms. Wilson, my name is Detective Miller—John Miller—can you tell me what exactly happened out here?"

She took a few seconds to look over the man. He was tall, she could tell that much. He was built for running, thin, but athletic. His hair was the color of sea sand, white-walled around the sides like a soldier, his eyes tough and calculating, dark as coal. But he gave off a gentle easiness about him, caring, almost fatherly. He had to be in his mid-40s from the lines of history etched into his face.

"It was a patient..." she trailed off, watching a stretcher come down the steps leading from the hospital, making its way to the ambulance, one of the many that sat in the courtyard. A bloody sheet with a mound of limbs and other pieces of faculty sat heaped and jiggling like jello mold as it was pushed forward.

"A patient, yes. What was his name, Irene?" he used her name, hoping to draw her attention back up to him.

He couldn't get over her beauty. She had a positively beautiful complexion, though marred with the horror she had witnessed. Long dark hair the color of copper and walnut hung down over her face. He could imagine it pulled back, or done up it some fashion. Her eyes were a starry blue, big, round and hurt. She had a strength coming off of her, he found it stimulating. She looked no more than a day over 30, and that was speculative.

"His name," her voice was sensual, he thought, "was Albert...Albert Walker."

The detective turned back to his partner, Simms, who was busy going through a pile of slop near the entrance where he initially found him. "Have Julie run the tag on Walker, Albert Walker, see what we can come up with; see maybe where he might be headed."

"On it—"

"Wait," Wilson said loudly, startling to the two men. "We're not sure if that is his real name or not... he never really divulged much. Doctor Grant believed it was a cover, maybe a man he killed back east somewhere, we're unsure.

Detective Miller looked into her eyes, again they were distant, playing out the events of the night, he was thinking.

"Simms, have her run it anyways, could get us something."

With that, Simms walked to his car, dropped inside and went for the radio.

"Ma'am, can you let me in on some of those things you're thinking in there, tell me how it all went down tonight?"

She looked into his eyes, then set about telling him everything. Every grisly detail. Even telling him about Albert, what she knew of the man, if man he indeed was. Told him how Grant had become, what she thought he may have been up to, even crazy ideas of what he believed Walker to actually be: some ancient beast said to haunt old lands, collecting heads and eating the young and old alike, but had an affinity—and appetite—for youth, the younger, the better. Even explaining in detail that horrible cave he had carved below, the Witch Hole.

He wrapped her in a blanket, guiding her to his cruiser. She sat back, a cup of coffee was placed into her hands from Simms who came walking up to the car.

He then made his way around to the driver side, Miller was standing about, both of them talking in hushed voices, deciding on plans of action, when Miller ducked his head back into the car and said, "Ms. Wilson—Irene—what did this man look like?" an urgency in his voice.

Again, she told him what he wanted to know. His eyes lit up at the description.

"Dispatch received a call around 30 minutes ago, telling Simms a man was spotted in the burb of Court Springs, acting funny, walking amongst the houses, matching the characteristics of this Walker."

She looked around in a daze, her eyes rolling around. Dreadful thoughts came to her, things she didn't want to think about. Court Springs, she knew it well. Drove by it almost daily, it was full of *children*. As if she came to a startling revelation, her eyes two wide bloodshot pools, she looked over to the two detectives and said, "We have to go, now!"

"I know you have the potential to be valuable to us Ms. Wilson, but I'm not so sure it would be a good idea for you to tag along—the mans dangerous, just look at this mess around here."

She sat forward, turning to Miller as he clicked on his seatbelt, hands readying the vehicle. She tossed off the blanket, "I know he's dangerous, detective, I know that all *too* well, but I'm *going*."

He knew there was no arguing with her. Ms. Wilson had to see this to the end, had to know that Walker, or whatever the hell his real name is, was put down—like a rabid animal. He also knew he wouldn't be going home anytime soon, something bad tickled his skin.

The two detectives swung their vehicles around the courtyard, bypassing emergency workers and uniformed officers, heading down the single lane road, down through those dark woods.

"I see something funny over there."

"Where?!"

"Over there, its...its, oh...*oh my God!*"

"*No, not again...*"

A luminous form, elongated, its mouth dripping in wide teeth, was emerging from the sink. It spilled out of the faucet in a drooling incandescence. As it continued to pour out in ethereal ribbons, its form gradually inflated out, two dead eyes staring into the kids with hunger, its gills flapping for air, the teeth gleaming in the light of the kitchen.

"*Run!*"

But it was too late. Ghost Shark struck once, then twice, the kids tossed about the room, torn to a heap. The parent's rushing into the kitchen from the agonized screams, tears streaking their petrified faces at the site of the children lying in a pile of themselves. The father looked up, and took notice of the giant, ghostly apparition above him, screamed as it came barreling down towards the camera, the width of the mouth closing the film in a black screen of rolling credits.

"That was awesome!" Michael said, lifting himself from the ground, standing up and making for the next movie, *The Basement.*

"It was pretty good, *I guess*. I was hoping for more blood, but it was fun," said Robby, stretching out below the glare of the blue screen.

"Wait, did they ever say how the shark became a ghost? It wasn't clear to me," Macy asked, confused with the origin of Ghost Shark.

"Who cares? It was awesome! Now, on to...*The Basement,*"

"What was that?" asked Robby.

"What?"

"That voice '*The Basement*'?"

"Haven't you ever seen late night Monster Mania, the host, Freddy Wolf?" asked Michael.

"You did *not* sound like Freddy Wolf, you

sounded like an idiot."

They both laughed, "okay, well then you do better," said Michael.

"How about we skip the impression and just watch the next movie?" said Macy, growing tired of their back and forth.

"Okay, okay."

Michael continued to his dresser, on top sat *The Basement*. As he reached out to grab up the case, something caught his eye, some shadowy outline of a man, skulking about the patch of garden his mother kept, just under the shade of a small pine.

"Hey, you guys..."

His words caught in his throat when he noticed something peculiar about the man in the dark. He seemed to be squatting, his arms running down his chest, his hands placed in the soil, his thighs spread wide to accommodate. His head appeared to be glancing towards the sky, slowly moving side to side, as if sniffing the air. Another feature grabbed him by the nerve endings, the mans eyes looked as if they may be glowing, he wasn't certain if the porch light below may be reflecting off his irises, similar to how red-eye occurs at the flash of a camera bulb, but it was a little unnerving.

"I think, I think I see somebody down there..."

"What are you talking about?" asked Macy.

She sidled up next to her brother when she pushed him aside and took a glance out into the backyard. "It's kind of hard to see, where was he?"

"What do you mean, he's right..."

The man was no longer there. His eyes searched around the expanse of the yard, still there seemed to be no sign of the shadow. *Maybe I'm seeing things*, he thought.

"I swear there was a man down there, out in the garden."

"Are you sure?"

"*Yes*! I'm not messing around…"

Michael turned his head back to the yard, studying the night. He felt a cold shiver worm its way up his spine at the thought of some stranger in their yard, crouched and ominous, shadowed like a specter. And those eyes, alive with a bloody neon.

"Maybe you're just seeing things," said Robby, who now brought himself alongside Macy and Michael. He cupped his hands around his face and pushed closer to the window pane, blocking out the interior light of the bedroom, hoping to grab a better look of things out in the darkness of the yard.

He scanned down below from the BBQ to the fence line, under the tree and around the garden. His eyes landed on the shed, "how about there, in the shed?"

Macy and Michael looked to the shed, from what Michael could tell, the lock appeared secure…on closer inspection, "*Wait*…Macy, *look!*"

She did. The silver lock was gone, on the ground just below the shed door, the metal clasp was flipped back, as if someone entered the structure.

"*Dad!!*"

Two minutes eclipsed since his scream sent his

father bounding up the steps two at a time, Stephanie close behind. To him it sounded as if his son was in distress, maybe someones hurt up there. He couldn't remember a sound like that ever leaving his sons lips.

Michael explained what he thought they he had seen out in the yard. Macy and Robby didn't have much to add, other than Michael appeared spooked after what he claimed to see out back. Thomas immediately dismissed their ramblings as nonsense, attributing their scare from those ridiculous creature flicks they liked so much.

"I'm sure its nothing, guys. You're minds are making stuff up; seeing glowing eyed shadows," he laughed, "you three need to watch less of this trash, its doing nothing for you," he told them.

But when Michael pointed out the lock lying in the grass, Thomas' eyes lit up, he couldn't remember leaving the lock unsecured, he was certain that he snapped it back into place earlier in the night. Of course he wasn't about to admit as much, telling his son and daughter and Robby that he may have forgotten to lock it back up when he was done messing around in there from before.

"Maybe you *should* check, Thomas," Stephanie said, a hand resting on his shoulder.

He turned to face her, she looked a little spooked herself. The thought that her son spotted some person moving around out there, the lock in the grass, something didn't feel right. Michael wasn't one for spinning lies often, especially ones involving shadowy figures in the night.

"Babe, I'm sure its nothing," he assured her.

"Well, if its nothing, please just go out there and check. For the *kids* sake."

And my sake, she thought.

He looked at her deeply, he couldn't say no. She looked truly frightened, he was unsure why, in his mind nothing was out there, why would she look as if she herself spotted some strange person. His eyes fell to the kids, Michael was looking up at him, waiting for a response, hoping his father would agree to sweep the shed, confirm he hadn't seen what he thought he saw out there. Robby and Macy, both had their faces pressed tightly to the glass, keeping an eye for anything unusual outside.

Looking back to his wife, her hands on her stomach, an instinct he knew she regularly used when feeling stressed, he grabbed both her shoulders and said, "Okay, babe, for you... and *them*."

A rare smile pulled her lips up, "Thanks, sweetheart."

She was hoping tonight she could get over the stresses, maybe release some with her husband. It was a difficult obstacle to surmount, events spiraled once they returned home and the kids made for their room. Voices grew in octave, tempers increased blood levels, words were exchanged with cruelty, later rescinded with eased emotions, tears licked cheeks and lips drew together in embrace. She felt amazed with Thomas. He genuinely appeared to want to make their relationship work, just as she hoped. But still, something nagged like a parasite in the membrane of her mind. She felt as if some things would never be disclosed, secrets that would take the bridge from under them, casting the pieces into the white caps below.

A flashlight gripped in his hand, the beam spearing a cone over the grass as he padded over to the shed. Up in the window he saw the waiting faces of the three children looking down on him.

He flashed them a smile.

Reaching out he took the iron handle and pulled the door towards him. The sound caused his own nerves to jump, like the resonance of opening an aged crate, or sarcophagus, scratchy, the springs inside rusted. Spooking himself, he let our a slight chuckle.

Damn kids have me jumping with this nonsense.

A slight hesitation gripped him before stepping into the blackened shed. His light knifing through the dark. Tools and bags of soil, used rags and lawn equipment sat jumbled and piled tight, no shadow people or boogiemen.

"*Kids!*"

Michael slipped open the window, "Dad, are you okay?!"

"Come down here."

"What is it honey?" Stephanie said. She was on the patio the whole time, watching her husband slink across the yard. To say she felt uneasy about the whole thing was putting it mildly, something stank, and it ran through her bones and chilled

71

her flesh; still thinking about what her son believed he saw. She always hated chiller flicks, something about the dark outline of a masked killer, a butcher knife raised above them, or an ax wielding counselor chopping out chunks of campers in some remote forest. She hated it. And now her son is speaking about things in the yard with glowing eyes peaking out from dark corners, sniffing the air.

"*Honey?*"

She continued to walk over as the three kids came pouring out of the house, their feet kicking through the grass. They stopped just before the opening of the shed, "Dad?" It was Macy, her voice small and gravelly. It was dark in there, *where did the light go,* she wondered.

"*AHHHHH!!!*"

"Dad! That was *not* funny!" Michael said, holding onto his chest.

"*Thomas!*" Stephanie had a hand over her mouth and one resting on her stomach.

Thomas was rolling with laughter, Robby too, was bent over, beside himself, pointing and laughing at his two friends who were rigid and bone white with fear.

Laughing some more, Thomas said, "I'm sorry sweetheart." Turning to his kids, "thats what you get for making me come out here in the cold, checking on your little boogieman out here!"

Michael was still standing with a hand clutched across his chest, "Dad you scared me half to death!"

"Me too!" Macy said, her hands up, placed on each

side of her head.

Robby continued to laugh.

"Thomas," Stephanie said, a smile on her face, now that the scare had drifted away, "please don't do that again, I think I aged a little bit at that."

"Ah, nonsense, you're as pretty as you ever were," he said, walking over to her, his hand guiding her back towards the house.

Her face flushed.

"Okay kids, everybody back inside," Stephanie said.

"Ah mom, can we stay out just for a little bit?" Macy asked.

Michael was standing back, his head dipped inside the shed, looking on things. He could hear Macy asking about staying out a bit longer, but something didn't feel right. He knew what he saw, and to him, it *wasn't* funny.

Somebody was out here, or at least they had been.

Looking down past the shed, a small dirt path led to the grassy yard, he noticed footprints, not his own, and definitely not his fathers. These were bare feet, the toes were clearly outlined, the heel depressed a into a ball of soil, the size much larger than his dads foot. His eyes widened as he went to mention the prints. He turned to face the house, catch his dad before he disappeared, when the blood drained from his face, his mouth locked open, piss saturated his crotch and ran down his legs. Above, in his bedroom window, two blood-red eyes stared down at him, lips pulled back revealing teeth as sharp as knives and long as fingers gleaming grimly off the moonlight.

◆ ◆ ◆

"So Grant believed this Albert was in actuality a legendary beast from history?" Detective Miller asked, his eyes on the road, the car accelerating over the limit to reach the place the strange man was last reported.

"Yes. I know it sounds bizarre, detective, but I'm starting to believe it."

"And why is that, Ms. Wilson?"

"It's hard to put a finger to it other than you had to see the man, know him, work around him. The way those men were torn apart, Grant...his *face*. It was awful. No *man* is capable of that."

"You'd be surprised what someone under the influence of certain narcotics are apt to do. We had an incident a ways back of a man we found talking to himself in an alley, the man was scratching at the brickwork of a building, apparently been going at it for some time. When we called out to him he didn't respond, just kept scratching. It was when we pulled closer to him we noticed that he had worn the skin down around his fingers, he had little more than skeletal digits at that point. It was later ascertained through blood work that he was percolating with methamphetamines; told us he'd been clawing at that wall for hours by that point—no pain on his face whatsoever..."

"Sorry detective, but I don't see what that has to do with a man tearing limbs from other men and those marks on the door. After seeing those rips up close, I'm certain they weren't caused by some tool or weapon of sorts, besides, Albert was never administered anything heavier than sleep sedation."

"What are you insinuating, Irene, that Albert is indeed some sort of monster? You actually *believe* that?"

"I don't know..."

And she didn't. For months now she had been watching Albert closely, the changes to the sanitarium, to Grant. They all seemed to coalesce, drawn together by some mischievous force. She felt it in her bones, especially when wandering the catacombs, she could swear at times Albert's voice carried into her, feeling around her thoughts, influencing lonely nights in bed. She developed anxieties over the whole thing, she wanted desperately to shake these mental images, but something blocked her attempt. His face would come to her in dreams, nightmares, horrible phantasms of her running naked amongst wet lands, a galloping demon on her heels, snapping at her from misty woods. She would refrain from speaking of these encounters lest she be admitted to a padded cell herself.

"Irene?"

Ms. Wilson, turned around. She had been staring

out the window since his last question, tears forming in the corners of her eyes.

"Yes? Oh sorry...I,"

"Are you okay," the detective asked, his eyes falling on Irene and back to the road. Something was eating her up, he could see that much. He figured he'd press the issue later, if time permitted. So he changed the subject, "how long you been living out here now?"

She turned to Miller, the tears drying up. She wiped her eyes, cleared her throat, and said, "Oh, around 5 years."

"Where you from anyhow?"

"I lived in Montana most of my life. After finishing school down there I received a call for a position at Blue Ridge, and well, that's where I've been ever since. How about you, detective?"

"Oh been going on just a push past 40 now. Been here all my life, plan on keeping it that way, too."

They spoke back and forth, busying themselves with common questions, she believed it was for her benefit, something to keep her thoughts away from bloody stumps, headless children and piles of gore.

It had been a good twenty minutes when the little housing community broke through the thick brush ahead, spilling along a narrow valley, bordered by thickets of pine. Detective Miller continued to speak, rambling on about experiences as a boot to climbing the ladder to homicide, she was paying little attention at that point. Instead, staring below, shuddering inside. She knew he was there, somewhere down there, she could feel him. Sense him, as much as she wanted to be far away from that man, she had anticipation growing inside of her. It licked her mind something awful.

◆ ◆ ◆

Their hands twisted and turned, struggled to loosen the thick cord of knots that bound their wrists together. Both laid up against one another, their backs coated in sweat. Their eyes bulged with terror and pain, tears threatening to release the adhesive compound of the layer of tape stretched across their lips. They thrashed around on the sofa in protest.

Below them, out of reach on the opposite side of the living room, Robby, Michael and Macy, lie side-by-side, their feet and hands wound in a nest of rope and tape.

Robby was unmoving, as if asleep. He'd been the first one to run into the thing in the house.

Michael pleaded with his father not to enter the home, that something was looking at him up in the window, something with child eating teeth and eyes that burned like hot coals. Again, Thomas was unbelieving, until they all entered the home, searching, more casual scares from his father causing jumping responses.

It ceased to be funny no longer when the scares

became real, the giant in their home tossed them around like dolls, dragging them into the living room, taking them one at a time from dark corners. Robby still hadn't come awake, they weren't so sure that maybe something inside him broke, caused him to slip into a coma or worse. They remembered him screaming out of sight when he was alone in the hall, a nail biting scream that diluted the color of their faces. Thomas could remember going after him, only to come tumbling down the stairs, arms and legs whipping around.

Michael and Macy were next, taken from behind Stephanie, leaving her alone, screaming and wailing, her hands enclosed around her belly. It was then she felt a hot, heavy breathing, a foul odor; some noxious wind lapping the back of her neck. She turned and swallowed. It was a man, a towering man, something looked sinister about his eyes, his face, like a patchwork of scars, a terrible suturing as if his face was cracked; a fissured web of bloody knife cuts.

Then her world went black.

Her vision slowly came back, minute details of her home materializing in shapes around her. She felt something heavy, she had limited control of her body, her hands were immobilized, she couldn't move.

That's when she realized she was bound to her husband. Thomas was unmoving. It took several deep pinches of his skin to bring him to. He became startled, trying his damnedest to release himself, pull himself up, anything to break free and go after his kids.

He realized they, too, were tied up, unable to move. Their eyes were wide, their screams cut off, tears flooded rivulets down their faces. He noticed Robby on his side, curled up, not moving.

"I see that you're awake."

Thomas stopped thrashing about when the voice cut into him with a poisonous feeling. Some dreadful timber caused his spine to stiffen up, the hair along his neck ridge to spike, his flesh pimpled in goosebumps. His profuse sweating caused the tape to give, the edge dog-eared, he dropped his head to the cushion next to him, wriggling his face along the fabric when the tape caught and peeled off.

"Who the fuck is there? Where are you!?"

"No need to get angry, especially in front of the lady."

Stephanie saw him first. As if a shadow, Albert drifted into the living room. His face still pieced together like a macabre puzzle, as if he hurried to cover his appearance up in some grim fashion. He kneeled in front of her, his hand reached up and ripped away the tape.

"What do you want!" Stephanie screamed in his face, the veins in her neck corded and tight against her skin.

Michael and Macy looked on the man with something akin to gut churning horror and madness as he drew closer to their parents.

Albert began touching her, his hands working

over her face.

Thomas continued to struggle, his head snapping back and forth in frustration, "don't you touch my wife you sonofabitch!"

Albert ignored the man, his fingers drawing down the neckline of Stephanie's shirt. Her face was a death mask, drained of life. A detestation of this man washed over her, claiming her. She began to shake and cry, stabbing yelps punctuated with each touch of the mans fingers against her flesh.

He paid little attention to the screams and yammering of the husband, the children on the ground, their grunts and sobs choked behind the barrier of tape.

With a rough pull, Stephanie's shirt was discarded to the ground. Her breasts exposed, her nipples hard. The man paid no attention to her chest, instead, his hands moving down to her belly. Both hands now, cupping the slight bulge of skin caused by the way she sat. His lips pulled back in a snarl, his eyes widened with hunger, his teeth seemed to shine and bleed around his gum line.

"*No...*" she choked, a pathetic whine. "Please... no...*please, don't.*"

"Leave her alone you motherfucker, you touch her and I will fucking *kill* you!" Thomas was fuming, his face like a boiler needing to vent. His thrashing grew more desperate. "Leave us alone, get out of my fucking house!"

"Don't worry... *Thomas*, is it?"

"*Fuck you!*"

Albert smiled, or what could be considered a smile spreading across those bloody patches.

"Don't worry, Thomas, I'll take *good* care of her."

"Please, don't hurt my wife, please... leave us alone."

"I didn't come here for social reasons," Albert said as he stood up, looming over Stephanie. He moved over to the children.

"What do you think you're doing, don't you *touch* them!"

"I want you to look," Albert began. "I want you to *watch* what I'm about to do, I want you to *remember*, to see it, over and over."

"What...I..."

As if stunned, captivated in some horrid lucid nightmare, Thomas did watch, Stephanie, too, as if enraptured in suspended time, watched as, like a wraith, Albert dropped behind Robby, sitting him into his lap.

Robby came awake, his eyes fluttering out the sleep. *What's going on?,* he thought drearily, his world fuzzy, his head a throbbing mess of pain. His lips seemed restricted.

Across from him, secured to each other, Michael's mom and dad, staring at him with blank faces. Robby suddenly remembered, albeit in a dizzying fashion, what had happened before his world was draped in black.

Something wet and moist, dropped onto his head, wormed down his face with a hot sticky feel. Above, Albert's face fell apart, those fleshy jigsaw like pieces broke away, spilling down his chin, dropping around him in doughy chunks.

Robby looked up, curious as to what was plopping down on him, when suddenly his scream caused his throat to go dry. A scratching baying bellowed from him like a wounded animal, as he saw what was above him.

Albert's eyes shaded over in that neon blood from before, up in the window, his teeth started to fracture along his gums; popping out in pearl slivers. New teeth, sharper, longer, thicker, began edging out, a sick bone grating sound followed each incisor growing down, his face too, started to change. His nose began to macerate like the rest of his flesh and fall apart, drawing out, pushing his mouth forward, his teeth now resembling hooked stalactites on the ceiling of some sepulchral cave, drool dripping off the tips, splashing along Robby's brow. Slanted ears unfolded and stood out menacingly, the bloody mask of tendons and veins flooded over in pooling layers of dark flesh, in its path a bristling of coarse hairs sprouted in thick bushels. His arms broke out, shedding its human exterior in great bloody flaps, consumed back over with that new skin and fur. It's hands ended in thick curving claws, black and sharp enough to cut steel. Both his chest and legs followed in contortions. The limbs twisting and forming with hideous sounds.

They all watched the metamorphoses in under a minute. From strange man, to something out of haunted books, late night movies, and misty swamps. A beast from faraway lands and tall tales, of legendary and forgotten lore, spoke about in hushed voices.

Stalker of man, devourer of children.

On the nights when the moon grows full and the howls shudder the strongest of wills, it hunts with a ravenous hunger. It had been called many things up to this day, but it will always be remembered as the *Beast of Gevaudan*.

Robby's cries cut off as the Beast drove its fangs into the top of his skull. His eyes seemed to glow brighter as the boy's brain wrapped around his teeth, the raw matter giving vitality, his stomach growling in anticipation. With a vice like snap, Robby's head cracked horribly in half, only his lower jaw remained with a flapping tongue loosed and lost without its home; a fountain of blood geysered up where his face used to be.

Michael and Macy were spastic, a palsy inducing a seizure. Vomit pushing up out of their mouths caused the tape to slide from their faces. Michaels eyes rolled over, Macy too, as they listened to the Beast feed on their best friend. Each sound driving a needling pain into their guts, knowing they were *next*.

The Beast continued to feed, ravenously. Disturbing vocals drifted out of its snout with each piece of Robby it tore free and swallowed.

Looking up to Stephanie, it tossed aside the young corpse and loped over to her. It's nose pulsing, sniffing, drool mixed with blood and skin dripped on to her, her face reeled back and fought a boiling nausea.

It's eyes seemed to show something beyond the glow, an opening to a world of pain and lands of blood. Her own eyes grew round, and she broke along her throat with a rolling scream that slumped her back into Thomas.

The Beast buried its taloned claws into her skin, rustling around her stomach area. Her belly was ruptured into a pit of hot gore, the claw dipped within pulled out a pile of viscera and organs, casting them aside. Then slowly... a small shriveled sack emerged. Something life giving, the *essence*.

As if in great triumph, the Beast stood tall, a great howl caused windows to spiderweb.

Thomas watched in abject horror at the thing standing over his wife, something in its hand, when he realized what it contained. He broke down in stuttering breaths between choked sobs and toddler like spasms.

"It *can't* be..."

He watched as that thing placed what was in its fist into that gaping maw, swallowing it down. Then something happened, it bound to the spasming children, scooped them up and over its shoulder, leaping through the picture window and howling horribly in the night.

"*Watch out!*"

Something with crimson eyes and moon colored fangs blew across the street. Detective Miller almost slammed his vehicle into it.

"What the hell was that!" he shouted.

Irene looked after it. It stopped momentarily, glancing behind it as if it sensed something familiar. The feet of two children lay exposed over its shoulder. It looked into her, its lips up in a scowl, showing those vile teeth.

"Oh God…"

It turned away and made up a slope in wide steps, ambling into the woods beyond the neighborhood.

"What is it Irene, was that it? Was that Albert!?"

"Yes…"

It was all she could say. Seated in the car, a million thoughts raced through her mind. *Doctor Grant was right, he was right all along. He knew it, why hadn't he kill it when he had a chance.* But then she realized why he hadn't killed Albert. The realization dawned on her in sickening waves. Grant wanted to *be* like him, to learn how to *become* like him. Maybe wanting Albert to pass along the gift to *him.*

"*Help!!*"

A voice muffled and echoing caused Miller to reach for his pistol, unsheathing it. He ran to where the voice cried out. Noticing the shattered window fragments glistening off the moonlight on the front lawn, Miller called out, "Police!"

"*In here!*"

Miller hurried to the front door, tried the handle —locked. "I'm coming in," he warned.

With a strong kick to the knob, the door gave, splintering along the side. Giving it a final nudge, his 9mm was up and searching. He arced the pistol up along the staircase following his front sight along the walk above that led to the bedrooms, "police!"

"Over here!"

Movement just below, on the couch. A man...and a woman, horribly mutilated. Robby's body was shadowed in the corner, hidden out of sight.

"Anybody else in the house?" Detective Miller asked, the weapon trained in front of him, probing unsearched pockets.

"No...nobody, please help my wife."

Miller looked onto the woman, she had to be dead, if not, her time was slipping. He reached into his coat pocket withdrawing a hand radio, "Dispatch this is Miller, I'm out at..."

"Where we at, sir?"

"...3...56 Alpine..."

"356 Alpine Dr. Court Springs area. I need immediate assistance. I have one down, something on the loose out here, get emergency here now!"

With that he dropped the radio back in the pocket, kneeling down to the woman. A cursory check of her vitals.

It wasn't good, her pulse was low, too low. She had a hole in her the size of cannon shot.

"Sir, please untie..." Thomas was struggling to

speak, the events sapped his emotional strength to the base, unable to draw on enough energy to speak, he uttered in fragmented speech.

With a knife he kept on him, he cut through the bindings. Helping the man sit back, to avoid looking at his wife.

"You...have...to...get...my kids."

"Where are your kids, sir?"

"That...thing, it took them."

Thomas took a deep breath, letting it slip slowly from in-between his lips.

"You...saw it, didn't...you?"

"Yes, I did."

Sirens sounded, drawing closer to the home. Blue and red flashes swam over the walls inside, highlighting the woman, casting her in frightening shades. The man, his eyes were gloomed over with a vacancy that was horrifying to look on to.

"I...didn't know...she was *pregnant*...she never... told me."

All the guilt of the past months he felt inside now broke free in a torrent of tears and pained wailing.

He lunged forward, grabbing hold of the detective. His hands clasped tightly around Millers lapels, twisting the fabric in his grip as he let his head fall into the detectives chest. His whining was pathetic and shrill. A broken man who lost everything and only now realized the torment he caused his wife and children. His lapse in fatherly duties, the times he cursed his wife for being a bitch as he pounded Jill in nameless hotels and dark parking lots. He wanted to die, *why couldn't it be me*. He wanted to talk to her, tell her how much he loved her, how he would promise to change, to confess and be a real husband to her.

"Sir, we're going to get you're children back."

Suddenly the tears stopped and he pushed himself away from the detective. Hands wiping tears. "I'm going with you."

"I'm afraid thats not—"

"—I'm going, whether with you, or in front of you, I'm going."

He had that same expression as Irene did back at the madhouse. There was no stopping a pissed off father and husband from hunting wild beasts and nameless creatures, nothing would prevent him from taking back his kids from that foul abomination.

It had been a painstaking, methodical search in the sea of woodland that bordered the community. A helicopter overhead flew in wide concentric loops, bathing the woods below in a ghostly illumination. Numerous flashlights in gloved hands bounced along steep inclines and under felled trees. Mega-phones shouted out the names of the kids in a static staccato. The moon continued its brilliance above, supplying the Beast with extra vivacity.

There were uncounted uniforms footing it along the brush, weapons slung over shoulders, some held fast in ready fighting position, searching tirelessly for the missing children. They were fed a watered down tale of a costumed man who had broken into a home, killing a mother and snatching away the kids and disappearing into the forest, armed. That's all they needed to know, it was enough to cause the officers to be extra vigilant and carry on; anybody who brought harm to kids was enough to fuel these officers with a seething energy.

Thomas was out front, his hands cupped over his mouth, shouting out for his kids to a quiet response.

Detective Miller and Irene followed closely, shoulder to shoulder, breathing hard with the woodland trek.

"What are you thinking?" asked Irene, looking below, avoiding the piles of forest debris scattered about.

"I'm thinking its like trying to find a coin in the bottom of the sea."

She knew he was right, but didn't want to say it. She felt those kids out there, same way she felt his presence amongst the shadows of the woods, could feel those eyes on her.

"*Michael, Macy*!!"

Thomas had been shouting and hollering for a good hour now, his voice was chalky and hoarse, nearly extinguished into a whisper. Tears lined his face. He was red with exertion, both physical and vocal. He wouldn't stop, not until his children were safe.

The trees around him stretched to dizzying heights, the sky almost swallowed up by the tight pine boughs above. He could hear the rallying cries and digital shouts with his son and daughters names bouncing hauntingly around the woods, as if his own calls to his children were mocking him from some alternate world. Taunting him. His legs were going to jelly, threatening to collapse under him. He wasn't built for this, even with the added adrenaline shooting through him, he was near the breaking point.

Suddenly, from above, splashes of rainwater poked his head, landing on his face as he turned skyward. He could hear it all around him now, the rain pattering through the trees, playing off bush and stumps alike.

"Just what we don't need right now," Miller commented, pulling his coat a bit tighter around his neck.

A low growling nearly startled him when he realized it was a brewing storm that was fast closing up the sky in a thick blanket of hazy gray cloud cover.

He watched as Irene cleared a denuded red pine, straddling then dropping over the other side, landing with a squish from the fast falling rain whipping a steady sheet down, saturating the grounds.

He followed, listening ahead as Thomas continued to shout that scratchy voice of his. Suddenly, he stopped as he cleared the tree.

Gunshots, several in the distance.

He went for the radio, "what the hell is going on, sitrep, now!"

There was a pause before a voice came back to him, "somebody got spooked, sir... shooting at shadows." As soon as the words left the officers reply, a volley of shots resounded through the woods, they were close, he could hear a whistling ricochet shooting off into the night. Several guns opened up when the same officer came back on the radio, "something *big* sir, something goddamn big just attacked my men. It took to the trees we're on its trail."

"Is anybody down?"

"Sir, oh God... Sorel and Jason, both down, bad, we need to carry them out now!"

"Mark your location, strobe your light to air overhead, copy?"

Static.

"Goddamn come back, copy?"

More silence.

"Anybody out there on this line—"

Miller nearly dropped the radio as what sounded like gunshots popped off around him caused him to pull his head down and squint.

Irene sank to the ground, her knees up to her chest, keeping small to avoid any stray rounds. Thomas continued up the incline, still calling to his children, impervious to the sounds of guns blowing off near him. "Thomas, get your ass back here," the detective screamed. He checked on Irene, telling her to keep low and don't move, he'd be back once he slapped some sense into Thomas. She did as instructed, too frightened to move.

Miller reached for his pistol, checking the chamber. Satisfied he had one seated, he held it low, his light up and forging a path in the dark, rain soaked woods.

"Thomas! Where'd you go, buddy, call out to me."

Shots were still ringing out, but with a diminishing volume, like they had expended their supply of ammo. A few shots were still scattered and far. Others uncomfortably close and erratic. That's all he needed now, to catch one in the melon from some boot who got spooked and took aim at any shadow moving about.

Screams broke out, replacing the report of gun shots just seconds ago. Horrible screams, caused his blood to ice over. Then more screams only seconds apart. He dropped down behind a wet log, the rain pelting off the bark in a steady rhythm. Only half a minute later another pocket of shrilling cries punctuated the rain, floating up his spine.

Then silence.

The helicopter no longer visible, its blades no longer churning the clouds, the comforting light no more. *What happened to them? Are they going for help? Maybe heard our shots and transmissions down here, unable to reach us due to atmospherics or some other work of science.*

He was hoping they had just went for help, but he had a long wait ahead of him for any cavalry to show up, he knew that much.

He could no longer hear the shouts of Thomas. There was an eerie quietness to the woods now.

His thoughts fell to Irene, he had to go back for her, get her out of there. He understood what had provoked all those shots and screams, just hard to admit he saw what he saw back on the road. Something that mythical to exist boggled the mind, it reset what you knew and what you believed. But the more rational, detective side, told him it was man in a costume who had seen one to many Wolfman flicks. And as much as he wanted to believe that to be the truth, he knew it was bullshit.

Men don't scream like that.

Whatever those men were shooting at got to them. Finished them. He didn't want to think about all the blood out there, being swept away by the rain, the bodies slowly sinking into the muck. He swallowed then stood up, afraid that maybe something with glowing eyes and black claws would take him apart. He turned and slowly descended the slope, heading back for Irene.

He was only a few paces left to where he had left her when a shadow moved off to his right flank. He took aim, holding his breath.

It was Thomas.

He was still calling to his children, a mannequin like face now, devoid of life, of blood. His voice was raspy and full of chalk, not even a whisper now came out of those lungs.

"Thomas," Miller whispered, lowering the pistol, his own breath shallow from fear.

The man was oblivious, didn't seem to hear Miller call to him, and if he had, he sure didn't waste time to look. He was locked on finding his children, so much in fact he could have walked right over them and not seen them. Something loosed itself inside him, he was a walking, emotionally disturbed, husk.

A hand reached out, wrapping around Miller's ankle, followed by a tinny voice, "detective."

Miller nearly jumped out of his skin, "Irene... Jesus!"

She wiped her self down from dirt, facing him. She noticed Thomas zoned out, ambling by like a zombie, detached.

"Oh *God*..."

They had their eyes on him, watching him cup his hands over his mouth, the cords stood out in his neck with whispered shouts. Then something hulking, bristled, with pulsing neon eyes and drooling fangs stood outlined in the shadow behind him. Thomas turned toward the Beast.

"Get out of there Thomas!" Miller shouted, the gun already coming up.

The Beast reared back with what looked to be a giant club of sorts, probably one of the smaller trees lying around in abundance, when Miller and Irene both noticed it wasn't natural to these woods at all.

Miller shown his light on the object and nearly caused him to vomit. Rigid as a trunk, Michael's body was drained, his skin looked aged and already decomposing. If there was an ounce of blood in that boys body, it would be nothing short of a miracle. His eyes were now black chasms, his mouth a dark hollow in perpetual scream. The Beast swung the body at Thomas, knocking him to the ground.

It then dropped with all the fury of a starving animal, its head twisting about in a frenzy; feeding on the man below him.

If Thomas was screaming, they wouldn't have heard it. The claws tore into the wet flesh of his body. Deep serrated openings pushed out organs and sent runnels of bloody geysers skyward. The Beasts' maw laid open a great gorge in his chest. It's eyes rolled back like a shark with each chunk of tissue it ripped free.

A sudden sharp crack sent the Beast skittering back, dragging the body with it, guarding its meal. It's back tightened and popped as it hunched down on all fours now, propped up on a log. It teeth drooling great ribbons of meat and fluid. It's eyes were alight with death, a searing hatred for the man staring daggers down the smoking barrel.

Miller couldn't bring himself to say anything, what could he say? *Put that corpse down?* Thomas was a fleshly mess, a bloody rag doll, dragged up the muddy slope by something that shouldn't exist. Some abomination of secret rites and myth, tired fables reduced to chasing big breasted bimbos around campfire lakes, not draining the blood of children and utilizing them like a common war club. Speaking of which, he said in a voice fighting for strength, "Where is the girl?"

The Beast regarded him with vacant, beady, man killing eyes. It's lips drew up, showing the mold of its gristly teeth.

Irene stood shielded behind Miller, her head peaking around, her eyes wide, the rain flattening her hair, dripping from her nose and chin.

It took notice of her, releasing a howl that shook the mud underneath them, vibrating up their bodies.

"Let us have the girl…" Miller said, his focus becoming more difficult to grab an accurate sighting of the beast along his gun, the rain splashing off the metal of the slide.

The Beast ignored them, lowering its jaws to the tenderized corpse of Thomas, working away slabs of skin and bone from his body.

A tuft of hair and bone along the Beast's shoulder exploded in a thunderous crack from behind Miller.

A police officer, a rifle in his hands, followed with another shot, then another. Both smacking the hard bark of pines, missing.

Miller grabbed Irene by the hand, dragging her along to the officer. It was a man he didn't recognize, but could tell was in need of some serious assistance.

His abdomen had been cut deep, a gash that was pushing out a steady sheet of blood ran down his slacks and onto the muddy ground.

Miller looked back to the Beast and noticed it wasn't there any longer.

Thomas' body was still slumped against a fallen

tree, his cavity emptied and hollowed out.

"What's your name?" Miller asked, his eyes up and searching the dark woods around him.

As the man went to answer, that horrible howl nearly ruptured his eardrums. He turned to look behind him and noticed it there. Only feet from him now.

It's arms wide and open, slightly crouched to match Millers height. It's mouth hung open. Ribbons of drool, distinguishable between the sheets of rain pouring down, dripped hungrily from its teeth.

Seeing it up close was another thing, almost mesmerizing to behold, some work of unnatural design, native to no land. And here it was, looking into him like he was a piece of meat. Miller's emotions went cyclic. He was unsure of what would happen, but he had a good idea that he would by lying next to Thomas if he didn't react, and quick.

He went for his gun, his hand working frantically around his waist. It wasn't there. It was *gone*.

His mind reeled, thinking of where he could have left it, when a sudden feeling came over him. A knob of metal caused the back of his neck to stiffen. His eyes rolling to the side, hoping to get a look behind him.

Irene.

His eyes drifted back to the Beast and he noticed something about *its* eyes, they were changing, as if speaking in subliminal waves, they pulsed, the glow increasing; thrumming with a neon vibrancy that spoke of blood and ashen lands.

It was the last thing he saw.

Another howl shook the trees and a single gun-shot rang out, muffled by neck tissue and plugging the barrel in brain and skull.

Miller sagged to the ground in a splash of rain-water and blood.

The nameless officer below started up, his mouth trying to work out a response when his words were cut off with another squeeze of the trigger, blossoming his face into a grim flower pattern.

Irene stood alone in front of the Beast, the gun hanging limply at her side.

Her eyes a pale glow, withdrawn into a fathom-less void. Her mouth slacked, the rain continuing to beat down on her.

The voices she heard moments ago were of a man, a man that haunted her dreams and worried into her consciousness. Encouraging her onward, to *help* him. And she gave in. Taking down the threat to that voice, such a hauntingly beautiful voice it was, pip-ing into her with silky pleasure.

It ambled to her, sniffing her, what could pass for a smile on that bloody wolf face pulled its teeth in a vicious show, and like a spring, it snapped over her head, tearing the stump of her neck from her body, dropping her next to the detective.

Her body flapped over the surface in a spasming death throe, thick scarlet waves pumped from the ragged hole between her shoulders.

The Beast stretched back, it's arms open, claws poised. It threw back its head to the moon and released a rolling howl that reverberated around the black woods, causing even the rain above to close up.

◆ ◆ ◆

It had been going on a week when they pulled out the last bodies. At least what they could find out there.

Some were simply beyond recognizable. Most missing limbs, nearly all missing their heads. It was a horrible sight. Hunters and officers, even elements of National Guard units, undertook heavy searches, going along every grid and overturning every leaf and rock in the area. The ones who found the body of a little boy voided their stomachs at the sight of him.

It was later counted they pulled out 23 bodies, one being the shriveled form of that child.

Curious happenings started to unwind that week, several kids in the community below went missing. Most last seen playing in the park when neighbors reported the children walking dreamlike up into the woods. Other times there were reports of a haggard looking man taking kids and dragging them into the pines against their will.

The community was in an uproar, demanding the authority do something about it. When they weren't quick enough, parents and residents formed armed cells and set about in search of the woods. Some of the parents started to go missing during these forays into the bush. People grew scared, hearing things at night, especially when the moon grew full and silver.

Some continued their visits to the trees, hoping to get their children back, but it was hopeless. There was no trail, dogs themselves were afraid to so much as approach the wood line, let alone sniff up into those foreboding patches. Kids drew pictures of the thing that took their friends up into the hills. One in particular that was reprinted and plastered on the cool metal of lamp posts around the area, walled up on street signs, had the title of *The Child Eater*, in scratchy, bloody letters; puddles of blood lay at its clawed feet.

Most sat at home, vigils sat silent in candlelight. Eye's peeked behind shutters and those that continued to brave the woods no longer returned.

Clawed deep under a pile of ancient logs, he sat, crouched in the light of low flames. It licked the underside of the mud ceiling in hissing whispers. His teeth worked the bones of children and men alike. Piles of leftovers covered in a tarp of flies sat mouldering and diseased. Blood spilled down his chin as he fed.

He knew they were out there, could smell them in those quaint homes below. He knew men tracked him, but they were no match, taken as simply as the children. He wondered if they would ever send another who could come close to routing him from his den.

One who would be able to finally put an end to, *La Bête*.

AFTERWORD

I always wanted to write an alternate world to the Beast of Gevaudan. La Bete. There is plenty of information out there in an array of books and a wealth of historical info flooding the internet. If you're curious, I urge you to look into the history of La Bete. Werewolves have always been a fascination of mine. I hope you enjoyed it, thank you very much to the reader.

This book is the first in the Splatter Fiend Series
The Child Eater- Book 1
The Shack- Book 2
Terror From the Sky- Book 3
Night of the Mutants- Book 4

-